this much is true

a novel

TINA CHAULK

this much is true

a novel

TINA CHAULK

Best wishes
Tina Chaulk

JESPERSON PUBLISHING

JESPERSON PUBLISHING
100 Water Street • P.O. Box 2188
St. John's • NL • Canada • A1C 6E6
www.jespersonpublishing.ca

Library and Archives Canada Cataloguing in Publication

Chaulk, Tina, 1966–
This Much is True / Tina Chaulk.

ISBN 1-894377-18-4
I. Title.

PS8605.H394T44 2006 C813'.6 C2006-902169-4

Cover photo: Stephen J. Tizzard
Editor: Tamara Reynish
Design: Rhonda Molloy

We acknowledge the financial support of The Canada Council for the Arts for our publishing activities.

We acknowledge the support of the Department of Tourism, Culture and Recreation for our publishing activities.

Printed in Canada

To Vince who always believed in me
and Sam who made me believe in myself.

And to Dad and Mom for everything.

Prologue 9
The Road to Hell 13
The Witch and I 27
The Cubby-hole 37
The Apps Bins 44
The Root of All Evil 51
The Rock 59
The Ugly Side of Love 72
The Ugly Side of Love Too 90
The Old Boyfriend 96
The Book was Way Better than the Movie 108
Best Laid Plans 116
The Grass is Always Browner 126
Baptism by Fire 140
The First Picture 158
The Second Picture 170
Sugar Pops 179
Raindrops Keep Falling on my Head 193
The Boston Jersey 206
The Be All and End All 220
The End of the Rainbow 231
The Big Move 242
The Long-Forgotten Sister 251
The Big Surprise 263
The Last Job 274
The End 283

Prologue

I am a good liar. I have known for years that I can lie my way out of most situations. I always have a plausible excuse when I am consistently late; I can fudge ten pounds on my weight (but I'm not quite sure anyone actually believes that); and my friend believes me when I tell her she can sing. It was only today, though, that I discovered just how good a liar I am.

My parents were always worriers, like I am now. One wrong turn of phrase, one sigh, could send them thinking I was depressed, extremely ill, bankrupt or, quite possibly, about to die at any second. So, how can you tell such people the truth? How can you tell them about your miserable job or your roommate from Hell or a terrible name someone called you? You can't, of course. And so I lied. After I moved to Toronto in 1983, I wrote home explaining how wonderful my life was, how fabulous my job was and how amazing the apartment I lived in was–well, it was amazing, but I told them it was amazingly good.

In the grand scheme of things, what is a lie? I know it is supposed to be bad. I realize that *honesty is the best policy* and the *truth shall set you free*, but what is the harm in telling a lie with good intentions? Okay, so, I know what they say about good intentions too, but I still think my lies were acceptable. Actually, I think I deserve a good pat on the back for my untruths. It was an admirable thing that I lied to my parents regularly for years. I'm sure, if they were alive, they would tell me how proud they were of the creative ways I protected them from the reality of my horrible apartment, rotten jobs and scummy guys.

I mean, it would have been wrong to write home and tell them how bad everything was. Dad would feel like he wasn't protecting me and Mom would worry herself sick and call me three times a day to ask, "How are things now?" So I told them how great everything was. Many of the letters I wrote them were not filled so much with lies, but rather they were carefully devoid of anything that was happening to me; more like sins of omission than anything else. Some of the letters, though, were heavily laden with falsities. But I still think I was being a good daughter when I wrote them.

I had pretty much forgotten about the letters until this morning when I went up to the attic of my parents' house. Mom passed away six weeks ago, three years after Dad died suddenly. With both of them gone, I decided to go up there and look around. In the corner I found a shoebox filled with my fabrications. As I read them, I recalled the truth behind the lies and felt a twinge of guilt.

My parents never knew what my life was really like those years ago, when I was away from home. At least I don't think they did. We can never be sure, I suppose, how much our parents really know about us when we only give them pieces of who we are, information dispensed in tidy little packages with as much or as little of us as we want to provide. I'll never know if they believed everything I told them. I choose to trust that they did and even if they didn't, they understood. A lie to protect the ones you love is not that bad. Is it?

The Road to Hell

Dear Mom and Dad,

I am in Toronto! It is amazing. I saw the CN Tower. I had a great flight up and talked with a nice woman most of the way. Before I knew it, we were here and I was on a bus to my hotel. It is hot here, but not too hot. It is wonderful warm, as Nan says, and I bet I will have the best tan ever. Don't worry. I know you think it is scary and rough up here but it's not. Going to Karen's tomorrow and will write with my address and phone number. Hope everything is good there. Take care and give Taylor a kiss for me.

Love, Lisa

Two hours before my flight to Toronto, I was on the bathroom floor of my friend's apartment swearing I would never drink again and crying because I didn't want to leave. My going away party included the stereotypical Newfoundland fare of fish and chips along with capelin roasted in the oven at 2:00 in the morning. There were also plentiful amounts of Black Horse beer and Newfoundland Screech, a fine rum named for our home and made in Jamaica. I'm pretty sure the combination of rum and beer made me so sick that morning, but I know the capelin and codfish didn't help.

It was July 16, 1983. I had just graduated from Memorial University of Newfoundland with a Bachelor of Arts and I needed work. For some reason, no one was beating down my door to hire a Philosophy major, so my employment opportunities consisted of waiting tables, clerking in a store or babysitting my cousin's two kids. Four and a half years of university made me feel overqualified for these jobs, but the four plus years of student loans meant I had to make some money.

My friend, Karen Keane, had been in Toronto for three years and my other two good friends, Jennifer Best and Kim Skinner, had been there for six months. Karen was trying to be an actress. Jennifer had put her Business Administration degree to good work at an accounting firm up there, while Kim worked in the computing department of the University of Toronto.

I didn't want to leave my beautiful island of Newfoundland. I loved the ocean and its beaches; I relished the waves crashing on the shore as they filled my ears with their roar, my nostrils with the scent of salt and my soul with peace. I felt at home next to the water, felt full of life when I looked at the beautiful vistas all around me and I didn't know how I would live without them. But I knew

I couldn't live without food and shelter. I had to find a job and leaving was the only way I could.

So I got drunk the night before I left and toasted Newfoundland over and over. The more I drank, the more sentimental I became until I eventually began to cry. "Why do I have to leave? I love this place. I hate that I have to leave," I slurred repeatedly. After a while, eyes began to roll and I started to hear, "Yes, Lisa, you love it here and you don't want to leave. We know!" I finally passed out, and somehow I don't think my unconsciousness disappointed anyone.

Lying on the floor of Joan Wellon's bathroom that morning, I knew I had to get up the strength to go to the airport. There was no turning back now. I had a one-way ticket and a place to stay with my friend, Karen. I had said goodbye to my friends, my mom, my dad and my dog, Taylor. This was it. Maybe it wouldn't be that bad. Maybe I would like Toronto. I knew one or two people who liked it. Granted, I didn't like those people and everyone else I ever knew who went there hated it and wanted to come home even if they stayed there, but maybe I would love it and thrive there, become a success at something and love the city life. Suddenly I had to throw up again.

I made sure no one went with me to the airport. I couldn't handle an airport goodbye. That would be too much. I would have given anything, I mean anything, to have someone run up to me and say, "No, it's okay. You don't have to go. You were offered a great job. I just got the call." No one did.

I turned and walked away from my home and down the long tunnel that led to the plane. A stewardess told me where my seat was. She looked into my face. Couldn't she see my pain? Couldn't she tell me to turn around and go back, that things would never be the same up there? She didn't. She just smiled and explained that my seat was in the middle on the left.

As soon as I sat down, the lady to my left started to talk. "Going to Toronto?" she asked.

Oh no, I thought. *I have a talker*. If she started already and asked me if I was going to Toronto on a direct flight to Toronto, then I guessed she would talk the entire trip. I wasn't a rude person, but I couldn't handle talkers, especially not when I was sad and missing home even before I had left it. Besides, even though I assumed there was nothing left in it, my stomach still felt like it had been turned inside out. My head pounded with every heartbeat. The fact that this woman would even speak to me was a testament to her as a talker. I must have looked scary. My shoulder-length brown hair, which had been coated heavily with hairspray the night before, now looked as though I had been on the receiving end of a massive electrical surge. As hard as I tried to get rid of the black mascara smeared under my green eyes, I still resembled a racoon. I was in no mood. This called for rudeness.

"Yes," I answered her, as close to her face as I could get and expelling as much putrid breath reeking of old vomit, beer, screech and cigarettes as I could manage. The talker turned green, then turned away. She tried twice more to speak to me during the flight. Both times I breathed heavily into her face and coughed. Both times she turned away and looked out the window. Once she tutted and muttered something about young people these days. At least I didn't have to listen to her during the entire flight.

Somewhere around Montreal, I fell asleep. I didn't know anything again until the stewardess woke me up to tell me we would be landing soon and to buckle my seat belt.

"I wouldn't wake you," the lady in the seat next to me said. "I thought you could use the rest after a night of drinking," she finished with her face screwed up.

"Thank you," I said, as close to her face as I could. She rolled her eyes and mumbled something about a toothbrush.

"We will now be landing in Toronto," the captain said. "Local time is 10:15 a.m. and the temperature is 32 degrees, but with the humidity it feels more like 41 degrees."

Forty-one degrees? I had just left St. John's where the temperature of late had hovered around 17 degrees. I accepted my fate; I will melt on the pavement of the airport. I could see the headline: NEWFOUNDLANDER DIES IN WEATHER RELATED ACCIDENT. "She never could stand the heat," a friend says of 22-year old Lisa Simms.

The woman next to me tutted again. The whole plane, made up mostly of Newfoundlanders, seemed frightened at the thought of this blistering weather. *This confirms it*, I thought. *I've left home and gone straight to Hell.*

I'm sure that when I die, if I am unfortunate enough to be sent to the fiery resort, I will already know what that first shock of heat feels like. I felt it after I'd gotten my bags and asked for directions to a shuttle bus to Toronto from a lady who seemed as friendly as a blade of grass. She told me to go to the eighth door on the left, where it was clearly marked that the shuttle bus would be departing every twenty minutes. Apparently, this clearly marked sign can only be read by unfriendly mainlanders since I looked and counted up and down the airport several times before finally running out through the nearest exit in a complete panic. I thought I was lost in the airport and would be trapped there forever. Panic left me as the heat struck my poor, cold-blooded, Newfoundland body. My clothes immediately absorbed every bit of moisture in the air and stuck to my body as if someone had vacuum-sealed them.

I began to feel faint when I finally found the little hut that sold tickets for the shuttle to Toronto. I discovered I would have to pay ten dollars to get to my hotel in Toronto. I thought I had bought a plane ticket to the city. Apparently not. Toronto was still ten dollars away.

I was in mid faint and leaning heavily on my suitcase when a man who didn't seem able to speak English very well said, "to 'otel?" and ripped my suitcase out of my hand to put it on the shuttle. If I hadn't been about to pass out, I think I would have put up a good fight for the suitcase. After all, I didn't know this man or even if he drove the shuttle. Mom and Dad had told me to be careful in the evil city. Anyone could rob me in the blink of an eye. However, I just gave up. He could have my suitcase for all I cared. I just wanted to get out of the heat before I became a puddle on the sidewalk. I handed the lady, the same unfriendly one as before I believe, my money and turned to get on the shuttle.

I had never really been air-conditioned before. I'm sure the Avalon Mall must have had air-conditioning from time to time in the summer, but I never noticed it. Air-conditioning was something that, if it happened to me, it was in the background and not really noticeable. That was until that day. My world changed suddenly when I got on the shuttle bus that would bring me to downtown Toronto. Immediately, I gave up worshipping God and the Trinity. My new god was the air-conditioner. I bowed down and thanked it profusely.

I got up off my knees and sat in one of the many empty seats on the bus. Well, at least, I thought, I would now get to see some of Toronto's sights. As the shuttle pulled out, I found myself getting a little excited. The CN Tower would be in my sight as soon as we got out of the airport. Unfortunately, it appeared I would never actually get out of the damned place. We circled, over and over around the airport, picking up passengers at different little shuttle huts along the way. Finally, after what seemed an eternity, I had a faint hope that I might see the world outside the airport. I did. Six lanes of traffic, a million cars (exaggerating only slightly) and the bus doing 140 km per hour. No Toronto yet, just Highway 401.

After a few kilometres, I could finally see the CN Tower off in the distance, blurry through the smoggy haze hovering over the city. It was a blanket of hellish heat. I like a little heat. I would have considered myself a sun-worshipper in Newfoundland, but that was with a high of 20 degrees. With a cool wind, it could get tolerable if you lay in the sun. Then the breeze would blow up and your goose bumps would get nice and tanned. Not so here. Here, the heat was constant–no breeze, no goose bumps–just sweat. Nevertheless, I was pleased I could see the blurry form of the world's tallest freestanding building.

We slowed a little and began weaving through the streets of Toronto. My stop was at the Royal York, very close to where my hotel was supposed to be. At least that's what the map said. Everything looked so close together and organized on the map. On the map, my hotel was down the street a little from where the shuttle stopped on Front Street. Of course, that meant getting off the bus. That required going back out there into the bowels of Hell. I stood there, inside the bus, for a long time.

Finally, the driver said, "You get off now. Now, you go."

I could have cried, but instead I nodded and, as slowly as I could, walked off the bus onto the street. There is a little known fact to those who don't live in Hell. It gets even hotter in the middle of the city. The windows of the huge skyscrapers reflect heat into the street so you get the same effect as being in, oh, let's say, a glass-melting oven. I discovered this pleasant little detail after stepping off the bus. Sweat poured off me and I was sure I would succumb to instant dehydration.

Needless to say, I was looking forward to getting into my nice, nearby hotel and an air-conditioned room, as promised in my hotel brochure. The brochure called the room 'cozy,' which I figured meant small, but that was okay. The price was right. Maybe it wouldn't be too bad.

I think that somewhere up in the heavens, there is a god of irony, especially for those people who think 'maybe it won't be that bad.' His name is probably Ha. Whatever his title is, his face lit up that day as I got off the shuttle. He probably jumped up and down with delight. You see, despite all the negatives, I was still trying–operative word here is 'trying'–to think positively about this whole experience.

The first thing I learned on the street that day was that maps of Toronto could be deceiving. I knew maps were done in scale (I'm not stupid) and I knew things weren't going to be as close together on the map as they really were. But this was ridiculous. The hotel that practically touched the picture of the Royal York on my map was, in fact, three kilometres from where I stood. I walked the whole way assuming I would arrive at the hotel at any second.

I was carrying everything I needed to live full-time in Toronto. I lugged three suitcases, a garment bag and two gym bags the three kilometres to my hotel. I did this in a temperature that, when you factored in the humidity, felt like over 46 degrees. I also swore every step of the way. The few people who saw me, those who weren't so disillusioned by it all and actually noticed me, must have thought I was a homicidal maniac. I swore and expressed desires to murder in very painful and inventive ways, the people who had made the maps; the federal and Newfoundland governments, who I felt were responsible for my being there; the shuttle driver for making me get off the bus; my friend for having plans so she was not able to pick me up; and every person who didn't get out of my way as I walked along. Everyone looked down and walked forward, oblivious to anything happening around them.

To be sure, there were things I could understand people not wanting to see. I found myself looking away from the homeless people on the street. It wasn't that I didn't want to acknowledge their existence; it was more that I felt guilty. I felt bad for not having any extra money to give them, but mostly for complaining about having to walk three kilometres with my big pile of belongings so I could get to my air-conditioned hotel. There's something about seeing the hardships of others that always makes your own seem so inconsequential. There's always someone else worse off than you, I'd always heard. I'd often wondered if there wasn't someone in the world to whom that would not be true. I whispered a quiet prayer that I would never find out.

Finally, my sweaty carcass, hauling my bags, fell into the lobby of the Hotel Suiteness. I collapsed against the front counter, manned by a seemingly friendly person. She smiled in the instant before she saw me; then, a look of horror came across her face.

"Are you okay?" she asked.

"I booked a room," I said, ignoring her stupid question. I was hyperventilating, soaked in sweat, had no doubt lost 12 pounds (not that that would be a bad thing), was hung over and was having difficulty standing. 'Okay' would not be the first word that would spring to mind to describe me.

"Your name?"

"Lisa Simms."

"Oh yes, we have your reservation," she smiled again. "Would you like to store your bags until 2:00?"

"Pardon?"

"Would you like to store your bags until 2:00?" She obviously saw my look of complete stupidity. "Check in time is not until 2:00." Again she smiled.

It is very difficult for me to describe exactly what happened at that moment. It remains a blur. I know that to say I was angry would require a new definition for anger and to say I was furious would be an understatement. I know I let forth several expletives I felt summed up my feelings at the time and burst into tears. The girl behind the desk–no doubt having seen numerous Newfoundlanders react the same way–just stood there, looking at me with a placid expression on her face.

"I'll give you a key to the storage room on the second floor. You can put your bags there and come back at 2:00," she said, seemingly unfazed by my reaction.

As she passed me the key, I hoped the storage room was air-conditioned. It wasn't.

I spent the two hours before 2:00 at a corner coffee shop. I drank three Diet Cokes and two lemonades. I read a local paper, but mostly I sat there, staring out the window and watching people move around the streets. There would be fifty people at a traffic light, all gathered around waiting for the sign to tell them they could cross the street. By the time half of them had gotten across, the sign changed to Don't Walk. They didn't mind. They all kept going. The cars also didn't mind when the light turned green. If people were still crossing, they had to move butt because these drivers didn't seem to care if the people were there or not. The cars came so close to hitting some of the people that for the first few minutes, I watched with my heart in my throat certain I would be chief witness in a vehicular manslaughter case. It was a strange dance of cars and pedestrians and I watched, waiting to see who would lose. No one did. Back home, I had seen people stop halfway across the street and turn around if the light changed to Don't Walk before they could make it across. That was with two people waiting to cross and no cars around. Welcome to the real world, Lisa.

2:00. I was back at the hotel to get the key to my room. I was disgustingly sweaty and couldn't wait to get a shower. The girl smiled, gave me my room key and once again gave me the storage room key. I got my bags out and returned the key to her again. I was almost there, almost in my cozy, air-conditioned room.

The god, Ha, was having a really good day. He'd taunted and teased me from the light at the end of the long, horrible tunnel. Not to sound too cliché, but that light turned out to be from a huge train. Its name, emblazoned on the front as it barrelled toward me, was 'cozy.'

Webster's dictionary defines cozy as "warm and comfortable: snug." Apparently, snug in Toronto means–and I'm honestly not exaggerating here–that when you open the door, you hit the bed. It also means the foot of the bed is two feet away from the bathroom door. The bathroom consisted of a stand-up shower, a sink and a toilet.

The one part the dictionary had right about this room was the part about being warm. Yes, of course, the air-conditioner was on the blink. I turned on the air-conditioner and sat in front of it, shirt open, waiting for cool relief. I offered a quiet prayer of thanks, eyes closed, to the air-conditioning god. I opened my eyes. There was nothing. At first, I was in denial and thought maybe I felt something. I sat there, willing it to cool me off, not able to believe what was happening. I then seemed to have popped a vein in my head as I vaguely remember calling down and threatening everyone's children if they didn't fix my air-conditioner or give me a room in which the air-conditioning worked. If they also would be so kind, I added, may I please have a room in which I could turn around without hitting a piece of furniture.

The manager seemed accommodating or afraid–I'm not sure. He moved me to a different room that was the same price, but a little bigger. It seems the rooms on one side of the building were larger than those on the other side. It wasn't a luxury suite, but it had a bathtub and enough room to move around. I stripped completely naked, bowed before the air-conditioning god and basked in its glow. I was in Toronto and I had survived the first day. Maybe it would get better.

Ha.

The Witch and I

Dear Mom and Dad,

How are you guys? Just a quick note to let you know that I am in a van with Karen and am writing you here so I can drop it in the first mailbox I see. I bought this postcard at my hotel and wanted you to see the nice picture of Toronto and the CN Tower. It looks just like I saw it this morning out my window. Imagine! Karen is great and says hi. She looks amazing, as always. Will write you again soon and let you know about the apartment. Hope everything is great there.

Love, Lisa

Karen, my old friend from high school, had gotten a loan of her friend's van so she could pick me up. I was supposed to meet her at 11:00 in front of the hotel. Check out time was 12:00. Not even 24 hours. It was 10:50 and the radio had told me only moments before that the temperature at the airport was 32 degrees with a 40 degree humidex rating. Ah, a nice, cool Toronto day.

I paid for my room and dragged my bags out onto the street to wait for Karen. We were roommates in university, in Squires residence, the two semesters she was there before she realized she had a calling to be an actor and moved away. Although we hadn't really stayed in touch since she'd been in Toronto, it was no problem because we were the kind of friends who could pick up after long absences without skipping a beat. I called before moving to Toronto and asked if I could stay with her for a while. I didn't expect the long pause before she agreed and it sounded more reluctant than I would have liked it to, but I knew it would be fine once we reconnected. I couldn't wait to sit down in her apartment, or rather our apartment, catch up on old times and have a beer with her. Come to think of it, I was just looking forward to having a beer.

She'd told me that she would be driving a blue Chevy van. God, who could know there would be that many blue vans in one place? 11:00 came and went. I would get excited at every blue vehicle I'd see in the distance. I got excited a lot that day. Excited and sweaty because, despite the stifling heat, I couldn't run back into the nice cool hotel lobby for fear I would miss Karen. So I sat on a suitcase outside and dripped.

Toronto, I had decided, was a city of toos. It was too hot, too big, too smoggy, too unfriendly, had too many stupid blue vans and it was way too far from home. If it wasn't for the lack of money and the shame at returning home without even trying, I would have went right back to Newfoundland. But finally, at 12:15, a blue Chevy van pulled up. I was sure it was Karen and I suddenly felt like everything would be okay. I would not feel so alone and out of place anymore. Something familiar and friendly was in that van.

My excitement grew as the door of the van opened. Then, I realized, I didn't know the person who stepped out. She'd sent someone else. The stranger smiled slightly and waved then started to walk toward me. I must admit I was just about to run the other way when I recognized that this was really Karen. I only knew her from her voice when she yelled, "How are you?"

She stood in front of me and shook her head as I stood there, in a mild state of shock, trying to figure out how the strange person standing before me could be my old friend.

"You haven't changed a bit," she said.

"Holy shit, who the Hell are you?" I blurted. I couldn't help it. I didn't know this strange person. This wasn't a tiny change; this was Extreme Makeover, the 80s edition.

In high school, Karen had been Miss Priss. Her hair was always perfect, always teased higher than everyone else's. Makeup was her life and I don't think I saw her without full makeup once in high school. Even when she'd stay over at my house, she would be perfectly coiffed before coming out of her room. She always wore the best clothes, clothes I could only imagine owning. She had Roadrunner jeans and real Levi's shirts, leather skirts and a leather disco bag. She had a black light in her room and about twenty cassettes before I even had a cassette player. She was the first person I knew to wear sandals, the good kind with heels, not the flip-flop kind. I had always envied her, not that she ever acted superior to me. She didn't. She was always kind and I could borrow any of her things anytime I wanted, but I wanted to own them; I wanted them in my closet.

Now the same person stood in front of me, at least that appeared to be the case. She was always a natural blond with silky hair I would kill for. Now her hair was–well, she had no hair, just black fuzz. Actually, that's not true. Most of her head was bald. There was a small growth of black whiskers around the perimeter of her head, something like what you'd see on Robin Hood's Friar Tuck. Her jewellery consisted of one earring; two rings in her eyebrows (one in each); a ring in her nose; and a horrible looking, I-feel-pain-at-the-mere-thought-and-can't-imagine-looking-at-you-all-the-time-wearing-that, stud in her lip. That's the jewellery I could see. I didn't even want to contemplate about possible adornments I couldn't see. Her clothes consisted of a thin, flared, ankle-length skirt, a black T-shirt and black sandals, not the high-heeled kind. She wore no makeup and looked paler than I think I've ever seen a person look.

"Are you a vampire?" I asked, considering it was the closest thing I could come up with. I felt comfortable asking her since we had always been frank and honest with each other. She was the one I would ask if I was gaining weight and knew I would get the awful truth ('cause, let's face it, you don't even have to ask if it ain't true). She felt the same with me. Somehow, looking at her and seeing the new person standing there, I felt the rules were about to change. I also knew that she had acted in a play the night before and thought that maybe she might have performed as a vampire.

"No," she said as she reached for my suitcases, not seeming surprised by the question. "Actually, I'm a witch," she announced without a smile.

She picked up three of my bags and started to march back to the van. I dragged the rest of my belongings along with me and realized the sudden fear I'd developed about stepping inside the van. No doubt I would be initiated into some strange cult, just as my father had feared would happen if I moved to the big city. Opening the door to get in, I was sure my fears would be proven right. Tarot cards lined the black interior walls; a red stain on the floor in the back set my imagination running wild and a plastic penis dangled from the rear view mirror. *Great*, I thought, *can't wait to meet all of her friends*.

We got into the van. "Thanks for coming to pick me up, Karen," I said, genuinely. "I don't think I'd want to spend another night at that hotel, although the air-conditioning was great. I think I'd die without air-conditioning."

"We don't have air-conditioning," she said, as if she were not destroying my newfound religion of air-conditioning worship. "Air-conditioning is only for the upper classes. It is a luxury reserved for the rich. I," she said as she turned to look directly at me, "am not rich. I am poor. And my name is not Karen. It's Rain. R-A-I-N."

I didn't say anything for a minute. What do you say to that? I was disappointed and a little scared: scared of her, scared of what living with her would be like and scared of living in Hell without an air-conditioner. What do you say to the person who went from Roadrunner jeans and perfect hair to a dark soul bragging about being poor?

"Oh," was the best I could come up with.

"How is everyone in Aspen Cove?" she said with a snide tone I was more than a little uncomfortable with.

"Same old, same old, I guess," I answered. "Maggie got married a couple of months ago. She was six months pregnant at the time. You can imagine now, Maggie six months pregnant. Her father went nuts and Bill Bememster had to marry her or I think he would have been killed. Neither one of them seemed happy at the wedding and poor Maggie was screeching to break her heart in the bathroom at the reception. And Christina Coish is pregnant, again. Her and Johnny just keep popping them out like they're Pillsbury crescent rolls. Sarah Peckford has cancer. The doctors only gave her six months to live, but that was a year and a half ago now. I can't believe that someone our age has cancer."

I suddenly realized I was rambling, not even pausing for a breath. I was afraid of what she was going to say. I thought, in my own judgmental way, I had her pegged. I'd seen her type before. She was against everything resembling the establishment and liked it better the more she rebelled against it. She would despise me and my lifestyle and, sure as Hell, would despise my gossip from home. She probably hated home as well.

"That's life," she said, "or rather that's death. As for the hometown crowd and their happy, domesticated lives, I left that behind. If all they want is to push out babies and be married to guys who wear gym pants every day and work a couple of months a year, then I can't even begin to understand them. Can you?" It sounded like more of a challenge than a question.

At the time, I wondered if I would ever like her again. She had already judged me, it seemed, and that was fine since I'd done the same. I had to live with this person and I feared how the story would end. We would live in tension and mutual seething hatred until we had the big, all out, never going back, I hate your guts, fight and parted ways. I wished it wouldn't come true, but that meant one of us would have to change. It was possible she would come back to my world, but there was not a chance in Hell of me moving into hers. I guessed the chances for her to move back into mine would be lessened by my presence around her and her need to rebel against "my kind."

"I've never been married or pregnant, so I guess there is no way I could understand," I said, trying to be diplomatic. "Whatever makes them happy." I'd try for now, even if she wouldn't. "What's new with you?"

"Everything," she began. Her story was interesting in the way hearing about what a plane crash feels like would be interesting. She had gotten a job at a newspaper in Scarborough a couple of months after moving up there. She'd partied a lot and soon felt she was missing something. Not thinking that maybe it might be homesickness, she slowly made her way into the arts community, trying out for parts in plays like she'd done in high school. I remembered her being very good. I'd wait to see what I thought of her acting in my more mature days of present.

After getting a couple of bit parts in some amateur productions, she'd quit her newspaper job and decided to never work again unless it was something she believed in and thoroughly loved doing. She would trade material possession for the pleasure of living a life of contented poverty and a sanctimonious disgust for the rest of us who didn't follow their passion. Small parts led to slightly bigger parts, and soon she found a small niche in performance art and eked out a living, mostly from government grants. She explained excitedly about her best-ever performance art role where she played a weed being crushed by a gardener who wanted a beautiful, natural garden. She found great irony in this and I could only imagine her writhing around on stage as a small, green annoyance.

Another performance, she told me, involved being covered in wet mud and lying under the hot lights long enough to let it dry. That was it. That was thc show. Her audience, who had paid eight bucks a pop, got to sit there for over an hour as the mud dried on her. Then, once sufficiently dried-apparently, there was a particular consistency that some guy came out every few minutes to check for-a man would crack it with a mallet. I pictured myself in the audience and knew in my deepest heart that there would be no earthly way I would be able to sit there without laughing hysterically. I could almost picture the audience sitting there, enthralled at her performance and reading deep, spiritual and ironic meanings into it.

Rain's current project was a masterpiece she had written about society's need to control people by making them work for a living. It was her ode to poverty again and I knew I would quickly grow tired of it, if I hadn't already done so. I didn't know what to say, so I just nodded my head and tried to be polite, hoping she would change to another subject. She did. I then wished she'd kept on the old one.

Next topic was the boyfriend: the man of her dreams who liked constant sex and believed in her work ethic. His name was Dreg. Poverty was his forte as well and it sounded like he did it well. He worked in a small garage band that got the scattered gig at a small bar or a wedding. Although he barely made enough to get by on, he refused to get a "real job" since he would only do what made him happy. He, I was told, did not wear gym pants, not ever. She explained that he generally wore tight shorts with no shirt, even in the winter, because he was tough and did not need the bourgeois trappings of clothes. He had, she said, a body any woman would crawl over broken glass just to look at and if I could find a way to smile through my abject hatred of him, I would laugh in retrospect about her description.

They lived together in a small apartment. This was something her mother had not told mine and I was pretty sure she didn't know. Regardless, I learned I would be living with the two of them and my day suddenly grew much worse. I would pay one-half of the rent and sleep on the sofa. They would sleep in the bed in the one bedroom–a sweet deal for people who loved their poverty. For the time being, there was little I could do about the arrangement since I didn't even have a job yet, let alone a way to be able to afford my own place.

Rain continued to tell me about her plays, her boyfriend and her group of friends, she liked to call her coven. Yes, Rain genuinely thought she was a witch. Not in the stereotypical sense, she explained, but in the truer, conventional sense. Witches didn't wear pointy hats and ride on brooms (no kidding, I thought). Witches studied various supernatural and philosophical truths. They met in groups and studied how to surpass the physical restrictions placed on them by humanity and the material restrictions placed on them by society. They could sense auras and send vibes, positive or negative, through the air. They could also sense powerful feelings, such as deep love and intense sadness. She said she sensed an emptiness in me. I wondered if she could tell that I missed my home and had a profound fear this whole thing would not work out. I'd left home to move to Hell and live with a witch and her half-naked boyfriend. I pinched myself, hoping to wake up.

The Cubby-Hole

Dear Mom and Dad,

How are you? I am fine. My apartment is beautiful. You should see it. I guarantee you've never seen a place like this before. My bedroom is pretty big with a double bed and a nice oak dresser. Karen even bought me a small chest for my bedside table. She is so good to me. The address is on the little business card I included. It is one of Karen's that she had printed up for her acting work. I know it says Rain Relante, but that is Karen's stage name. She is still the same old Karen. I will write you again soon. Give Taylor a kiss for me. Oh, I was talking to Karen's mom on the phone last night and she said to say hi and that she is so happy I am living with Karen and hopes I bring a bit of home to Toronto for her. She said she would probably see you at the dart tournament next week because Carmanville is playing in it too and she is on the women's team.

Love, Lisa

So far, Toronto was not living up to my already low expectations so I didn't have too much hope built up when I walked up the five flights of stairs to my apartment. I could hardly breathe by the time I got there. The stairs themselves had just about killed me and the heat had sapped every bit of strength and moisture I had in my body. I was ready to collapse the minute I entered the apartment. Collapse and breathe since I could barely get my breath.

Sometimes not breathing can be a good thing like if you are hiding from a killer and you don't want him to hear your breathing or, of course, being underwater or when you enter a tiny, 'cozy' apartment that smells like some kind of sadistic perfume factory the Nazis came up with to torture their poor victims. My new apartment was such a perfumery. Ah, yes there was the delightful new scent *Eau de Piss de Cat* and the equally fascinating *An Evening of Mildew*, but my favourite was the *Odeur de Dreg*. You see, Rain didn't explain that while Dreg wears only tight shorts all the time, they are the same pair of shorts, which are washed at the time of the winter and summer solstice (well, at least that's how it smelled to me) and are so tight because they are more or less stuck onto his body with old sweat and dirt. Factor into this Dreg's desire to wear no shirt and no deodorant because it is not natural to cover up your own scent with artificial fragrances the heat which felt like it was 40-odd degrees and no air-conditioning and you will get a vague idea of this particular scent. Dreg was not even in the apartment, so I did not know at the time what the smell was, but his stench hung over the whole place like a thick cloud.

When Rain saw my eyes watering, I told her it was because I missed home. The real reason for my tears was my physical reaction to the stink and knowing that this apartment was my room in Hell; picked out by the devil himself for some past sin I must have committed and could not name. This was worse than I could have ever imagined.

Until Rain showed me my 'room.' It was the living room and it included a sofa set, which was orange with bright blue flowers. All the legs were broken off so I had a new abdominal exercise: getting on and off the sofa. There was an old army footlocker in the corner. The coffee table was a big slab of concrete laid, haphazardly, on top of four old glass transformers. Rain proudly informed me that Dreg had made it himself. I wondered if the people downstairs knew they had this huge piece of concrete hovering above them, which, if it fell off its legs, no doubt would crash through their ceiling.

I could see the dining room was also furnished in post-modern whatever-we-can-find-to-use-for-free. It contained a chrome table with two chrome chairs (neither of which matched the table), one plastic lawn chair and an old rocking chair. I liked the rocking chair. It reminded me of the one Nan used to have, except we didn't sit in it at the table.

The whole apartment was tiny and reminded me of

the place under the stairs at my aunt's house. They called it the cubby-hole. A cubby-hole is a tiny compartment, and now I lived in one. Unlike the one in my aunt's house, it did not contain cool old books and an ancient typewriter I could spend hours banging on. My new cubby-hole was smelly and full of Rain and Dreg.

I quickly realized the sofa was the source of the cat piss smell permeating the apartment and wanted to scream at the thought of having to lay my ass on it let alone my head. I expressed, as calmly as I could, how I felt to Rain.

"No frigging way, Rain, am I paying half the rent to sleep on that. It stinks. The whole place stinks and it's hot enough to kill you. Dear Jesus, how can you live like this?" I said. Alright, I screamed, but just a little.

"Well, get your own sofa if you want, but we are not going to spend any extra money because you don't like our furniture. You are just too picky. There is no smell in that. That sofa cost us not one cent-we saved it from going to the dump when we found it outside the building about to be thrown out. The world is the way it is because of people like you who feel it necessary to buy new things all the time and support the big corporations who..."

"It was going in the garbage because a cat apparently died in it," I interrupted. "My God, you must smell it. And you must smell the other stinks here. It's awful. I can't even figure out what it is."

"It is probably our incense which we like to burn, and if you don't like it, you don't have to stay. I can't believe you're being like this. I even bought you that locker there so you could put your stuff in it and because I know how you feel about the war." She sounded genuinely hurt.

I think I was in a war in another life, probably World War I since it is the songs and scenes from that war that always bring a tear to my eyes. I talk about it a lot to people, especially if I have been drinking. I then have the annoying habit of lecturing people about their freedoms fought for by young kids who died over there and how they must vote and be grateful and for the love of God, can you not keep a poppy in your jacket or go to the Remembrance Day celebrations. I wear black every July 1. I know it is Canada Day to most, but in Newfoundland it is the anniversary of Beaumont Hamel, the horrible day in 1916 when 801 Newfoundlanders tried to take a German position in France's Beaumont Hamel and only 68 answered roll call the next morning.

Rain knew how I felt about the war and, in her own way, had tried to make a nice gesture. Yes, the locker was probably cheap or may have been lying out for the garbage next to the sofa, but she had thought of me and it did give me a place to put a few things. I knew my situation must have been better than whatever the poor bastard who had owned the footlocker went through.

"I'm sorry," I said. "I just miss home and this is hard for me. I feel like I'm imposing and I don't even have my own room. This is not what I had pictured. Not one thing is like I thought it would be." Despite my best efforts not to, I started to bawl–great, gut-wrenching sobs.

I sat on the stinky sofa and Rain sat next to me. She

patted my shoulder and said it would be okay. We talked. We talked honestly and openly for about ten minutes. She agreed she would help to have the sofa cleaned or, if I could find a really cheap used one that did not stink, would chip in on the price. She explained to me about Dreg's filthy (which she called eccentric) clothing policies and told me I would get used to it. She even found an old blanket in the closet and we used it to cover up the sofa so at least I would not have to directly touch it while I slept. After more crying, which by now I was using to milk everything I could out of this, she agreed that if I paid for an air-conditioner for the window, I could put it in the living room.

I found myself thinking that maybe this could work. Maybe it would be okay to live here and I would really get used to it. My hopes rose to the point that I smiled and asked Rain if she wanted one of the beers I'd picked up on the way there.

Then Dreg came home from rehearsal. He stood there in his grungy shorts and untied sneakers and, very obviously, looked me up and down. He smiled and nodded his head.

"Mmmm," he said as his eyes continued to grope my body. "I'll like having you around."

He then grabbed Rain by the shoulder and guided her roughly into the bedroom. In that moment, I decided I did not like him. I disliked the way he touched her. And if I'd listened to my instincts, I would have shoved his stinky ass out the window right then and there. Instead, I gave him the benefit of the doubt. Maybe Rain liked it a little rough. Who was I to say?

I opened up the locker and the smell of years of being unopened struck me. I started to line the inside of the locker with some scented paper my mother had made me bring. I was resentful of it then, thankful for it now.

As the moans got louder and the squeaking of the bed increased, I felt uncomfortable for myself and disappointed for Rain. I'd started hearing them not three minutes after they'd gone into the room. I got up and walked out of the apartment, not knowing where I was going and regretting having to return.

The Apps Bins

Dear Mom and Dad,

How are you? Things are going great here. I had my first night in my apartment and slept like a baby. I met Karen's boyfriend. He is a musician. I expect they will be famous soon and I will be able to say that I knew them when.

I am going to start looking for work today. Everything is so big here and there are so many buildings that my odds of getting a job are fantastic. I am hoping to see Jennifer and Kim sometime this week. Oh, I am so excited. This will be great. See, all that stuff you guys said about it not being a good move and that I would hate it here was not even close to the truth. I don't want to say I told you so but...

Anyway, miss you all.

Love, Lisa

The next day, after spending a couple of hours with the yellow pages at a corner coffee shop called Sweet Teeth, then returning to my cubby-hole for an uneasy night's sleep, I set out to find a job. After all, that was the reason I'd moved to Hell. I didn't have much money and needed to act fast. I had my résumés made up before I left Newfoundland so I felt like I was two steps ahead.

I decided to start by trying to get a job that had something to do with my degree. Not easy to do with a Philosophy degree, I admit, but it was a degree and that was a prerequisite for many jobs. It was 1983 and while there were no jobs in Newfoundland, this was Toronto and I had no doubt there were hundreds of employers just waiting for a young, enthusiastic Philosophy major to stroll into their office and take the high paying, very important job they had waiting for me.

My high school guidance counsellor had told me that in order to get a job you could not just send out applications. You should go see the person in charge of hiring so you could meet potential employers face to face and make a good impression. He said that when looking for a job you need to go door-to-door and bug people until they hire you. So, on day one I initiated the master plan to snag my dream job.

I took the list of promising employers I had compiled

at the coffee shop, got out my deceitful map of Toronto and set on my way. For the first day, I had a list of twenty businesses in the same general area of downtown Toronto, or so my map said. This, I was sure, would be easy.

I dressed smartly in a skirt and top. I felt my makeup was subtle but professional and knew the résumés I photocopied before I left for Toronto were impressive. They looked nice and said 'curriculum vitae' and not 'résumé' on the top. My friend with a good electric typewriter had typed it for me and I had made eighty photocopies at the university library in St. John's.

"Can I speak to the person in charge of hiring?" I asked on my first stop. It was an eighteen-story building and all the floors belonged to one huge exporting company. The person in charge of hiring, I was told by a woman who answered ten calls while I waited for her to talk to me, was called the Human Resources Department. A cold, rude woman at the desk in the HR department told me I could leave my résumé with her.

"If he's available, I would really like to speak to someone who does the hiring," I said, putting the women's lib movement behind ten years.

"Which you can do, if you get to the interview process." She passed me a piece of paper. "Please complete this application and include what kind of employment you are seeking."

"Well, what's available?"

"We do not have any positions open at the moment

but any that do become available are advertised in the *Star* and the *Globe and Mail*." She turned away and dismissed me by shuffling some papers around on her desk.

"But you can take my résumé, right?"

"Fill out the application first. You can attach your résumé if you want. Then leave it in that bin over there." She pointed to a plastic basket labelled 'Apps.' She then stood up and walked away. Unless I decided to chase her through the office, she had successfully dismissed me and I was frustrated.

I filled out the application quickly by writing 'see attached résumé' on every section then dropping it in the Apps bin.

The exact scene was recreated an amazing twenty times that day. I left twenty 'apps' in twenty plastic baskets and got to speak to a total of zero people in charge of hiring and twenty different receptionists with varying degrees of rudeness from "leave it in the bin" to "do you understand English? You will not get to talk to anyone in charge of hiring, ever."

I noticed that the receptionists looked harder and harder at me as the day went on. At first, they just looked at me like I was some naïve, annoying gnat. As the day went on, they each looked a little more horrified until the last couple of mean receptionists stared at me like I was some strange beast. Toronto, I realized, was such a cold, heartless place that people were shocked when someone showed up in person to try to talk to another human being.

The day ended at 4:00 in the hellish heat of downtown Toronto. I had managed to drink several bottles of cola, but still had not peed once; such was the mammoth amount of sweat leaving my body.

I walked into the cubby-hole, assessed the atmosphere and smelled that Dreg was not home. Even though his scent lingered after he left, it was more tolerable when he was not there.

I wasn't surprised Rain shot me a hard look when I walked in, but since it was the exact same look I got from the last couple of receptionists I'd seen, I went running to a mirror. It seems that humidity and walking around in 45-degree heat is not good for your appearance. The teasing I had done in the morning was gone and my hair was frizzy on the sides and flat on top. I looked like BoBo the clown. My makeup, which I had so carefully applied that morning, had melted all over my face so I had a very brown chin and black streaks down my cheeks where my mascara had run; apparently, waterproof and sweat proof are not the same. My clothes were soaking and would not be an attractive sight on the sleekest of women, let alone on my less than perfect body. It was sort of like wearing Lycra. Each and every extra curve and roll was more pronounced. I wouldn't hire me to wash dishes let alone to work in marketing or accounting.

I refused to cry again even as my bottom lip quivered and salty water filled my eyes. I mean, maybe people were vying for a hard working young woman with loads of imagination and talent, but no one would get to know me. I was an anonymous piece of paper with a list of work experience that included McDonald's and a Young Canada Works Project where I made picnic tables and fireplaces for a non-existent park. I needed to talk to employers to impress them and tell them how good I could be because I had not yet had the opportunity to prove myself.

I washed my face and went out into my room where Rain was burning incense and writing something in a spiral notebook. She asked me how it went and I told her about the rude receptionists and how I had not gotten to see anyone who actually does any hiring. She went into a long spiel about the impersonal face of big business and how I would be better off if I found something I really wanted to do, then figured out how to make money out of it. *Can I make money not living here with you and your smelly boyfriend?* I wondered to myself.

After a couple of minutes of silence, Rain piped up. "Well, one of the guys in Dreg's band, Remy, works at a place that manufactures cleaning stuff and he is always talking about how the head of the company loves to hire Newfs, as he calls us. Remy told me if I ever wanted a job there to just let him know."

I turned slowly to look at her. "Why didn't you tell me that before? You know I'm here looking for a job. That's why I moved here."

"You said very clearly on the phone that you were coming here to get a job in an office. Your own office, you said. Well, punching holes in a can of Comet doesn't sound like that, does it? So why would I think you would want to be told about that job?" She spoke softer than her words called for.

She was right. I remember I had told people back home that I was going to only work in an office and would never work in a factory. Just over 48 hours in Toronto and I was already willing to compromise my principles and goals. Of course, my ultimate goal was to get a job and now my other big goals were to get a decent couch and a little idol to the air-conditioner gods to put in my window. If working in a factory meant I could get those things while continuing to hunt for my office job, then that's what I'd have to do. After all, it was just temporary.

"Think he'd get me a job?" I asked.

The Root of All Evil

Dear Mom and Dad,

I have a job! Yes, I know it has only been one day, but Karen had a connection who was really interested in getting someone with some university under their belt so I fit the bill. Yay!

I work with a company called Windmere Packaging and they package a variety of cleaning products and other stuff. I work in the shipping/receiving department and I am the one who makes sure that shipments go out to buyers and come in from our suppliers. It is a pretty nice office job. It is a lot better than working on the factory floor where they package the stuff.

How about you guys? You okay? How is Jay? I miss her and her stinky dog breath. I hope you guys aren't feeding her too much. She'll be big as a bear if you let her eat everything she wants.

Love, Lisa

Sweat. Small word, easy to say, but my God it takes on new meaning when you're working in a factory in Etobicoke in the summer. I don't think I had ever really worked before I started at Windmere Packaging, packing up that God-awful Windmere Cleanser they made. I wasn't relegated to punching holes in cans, but I did get the wholly unglamorous position of tape technician. A tape technician fills the empty cases with cleanser, gives the cans a cursory inspection and then tapes the boxes shut with a handy-dandy tape dispenser.

Doesn't sound too bad, right? But, the cases came through at what you might call a brisk pace. Now tape is not a truly technical invention but it can get tangled up in itself sometimes, especially when changing rolls, and that's when the cases can pile up. You have to move fast and shut your brain off at the door. Not as easy as it sounds.

I am a daydreamer, a thinker, an over-analyzer of all things great and small, so not thinking is hard for me, especially when the task at hand is as mind-numbingly monotonous as mine was. Count, look, tape; count, look, tape; count, look, tape-hour after tedious hour. Sweat rolling down your face as you fear you might die from heat exhaustion (no air-conditioning here) and you can't drift off in thought for a second or you might lose track of it all. At least that's true in the beginning. After a while, it gets more routine and easier as you get faster. Your actions are so robotic and repetitive, you could almost close your eyes and still do fine (of course, you wouldn't really be checking the cans then). At least, that's what I was told. I never really got to that point.

My supervisor was a guy named Guido. Of Italian descent, he seemed to support the stereotype and expected others to do the same. He wore tight shirts open to his belly button, lots of gold rings, a bracelet and two chunky medallions on thick chains. He would jokingly ask people to kiss his ring or his ass, either way, and shrug when they did neither. He liked to hire Newfs because they were such hard workers. He also felt we should be the butt of at least two or three Newfie jokes every day. He spoke slower to those of us from Newfoundland, as if we could not understand this foreign language, called English, he spoke.

Many who hired labourers of any kind in Toronto shared his view that Newfs were the best workers. This made it very difficult for me because, well, let's just say that since they liked to lump us all together, I was dragging the whole lot of us down.

You see, I wasn't very good. Not so much not good, I guess, as terrible. I wasn't bad at my skill-testing job of taping boxes; it was my other challenging job of making boxes. Yes, I got to make the very boxes I later filled with a generic abrasive cleanser. I got to unfold the flattened boxes and staple the bottom flaps shut with a foot operated stapler. Sounds simple, but I found the whole process clumsy and difficult. While I couldn't really screw up filling the boxes and only occasionally screwed up the taping, I quite often got behind on assembling the boxes. It would take me three or four hours to make a couple of hundred boxes while some of my colleagues, unburdened by a useless university degree, could flick through theirs in an hour and change.

So I was slow and not so great at my job which, I feared, could mean an eventual turnaround in the reputation of Newfoundland workers. Soon, my supervisor's frustration with his less than spectacular Newfoundland employee would spread to other factories and construction sites. Before we could do anything to change it, employers would no longer hire Newfoundlanders, but would say "I don't hire Newfs. They're lazy and slow." I had to buck up. The reputation of Newfoundland workers rested on my tired, sweaty shoulders.

I wanted to be like the legend. I wanted to be like the man who could put together 350 boxes in an hour, a man who could fill those boxes and tape them up with his eyes closed. I saw him do it. He was a man known only as Ralph.

Like Cher and Madonna, Ralph had only one name. No one, no matter how many people I asked, seemed to know Ralph's last name. When people asked why I wanted to know, I explained that I wanted to talk to him about something and I wanted to call him Mr. Whatever. This always brought forward howls of laughter. Ralph, I was told, would hate to be called Mister. Someone had once referred to him as 'sir' and Ralph never spoke to him again.

I wanted to speak to Ralph about my poor work performance. I hoped he would be able to give me a few tips on how to do my job better. I knew the best time to talk to Ralph was mid-morning, after his first couple of drinks. If I spoke to him before then, he would be too crooked to talk to; if I waited until after he had too many, he would probably not be of much help to me. Ralph was what we would call today a functional alcoholic. He started drinking about three minutes after he clocked in (well, that's when he started drinking at work; I'd guess there were a few nips to get him going in the morning) and ended about three minutes before he clocked out. People took turns clearing away the bottles that tended to pile up behind the box stocking area. The weird thing is that Ralph did just fine with that amount of booze in his system. He never acted drunk, never had an accident at work and was always the top producer. I never saw him work without drinking, but I'm sure it wouldn't have been a pretty sight.

Guido loved Ralph and always turned a blind eye to the drinking. These days there would have been teams of counsellors from Employee Assistance Programs trying interventions with him and repeated suspensions until he got fired. I'm not saying that Ralph's drinking was right or wrong but it seemed to work okay for him.

So, at the 10:30 break on the third Tuesday I worked at the factory, I sat next to Ralph in the corner of the box stacking station as he drank from his brown paper bag. He was in grey pants and a black T-shirt, same as everyday, his own personal uniform. He had thick, grey hair, a bulbous nose and ruddy cheeks. He always looked like he'd just been out in a big gale of wind. Kind of short, about 5'5", he was thin everywhere except his protuberant belly.

"Hi," I said.

"Young Newf," he said, nodding to me and taking a swig.

I'm not really the type to go up to a stranger and start a conversation out of the blue, especially a fifty-something alcoholic I had nothing in common with except that we worked at the same place. Even that was more of a difference than a commonality since he was the best at his job and I was undoubtedly the worst. Still, I really wanted to stop hating myself and feeling guilty about how bad I was at this job. It wasn't my dream job, but I wanted to be good at it.

"Listen, I'm pretty shitty at his job and I was wondering if you could help me out since you're so great at it," I dove right in. "I was wondering if you could give me some advice."

"Sure. Don't use words like 'shitty.'" He didn't look at me. "They don't sound good coming from anyone, but especially not from a young girl."

He was right. Because he was older and drank a lot, I thought it would feel more like we had something in common if I talked like that. I should never assume anything about anyone. There is no doubt that people respect you more if you don't talk with a gutter mouth.

"Sorry," I said as I hung my head low. Whatever nerve I'd built up to speak with him was fading fast. "You're right."

Another swig. "Of course, I'm right." He turned to me and a hint of a grin showed in his creased face. "But you are pretty shitty at this." I nodded. "Why are you working here?" he asked.

"Same as everyone," I said. "Money."

"The root of all evil. I don't work for the money. Gives me a place to go and something to do that I'm good at. Plus, people leave me alone about," he paused and turned the bottle around in the paper bag, "stuff."

"I need money and this was the first job I could get. I wanted to work in an office but I figured I'd work at this while I looked for an office job."

"And have you been looking for an office job?"

"Well, I put in long hours here and I'm so tired after a shift. Plus, I'm working all day so I don't have much time in the daytime to drop off résumés."

My excuses sounded hollow to me and I suddenly realized I hadn't even thought about looking for another job even though I didn't like this one.

"Mmmm, there's always a reason." Swig. "I've worked here thirty-two years and I've seen at least a hundred kids come through those doors to work at this job until a better one came along. Most of them are still here. Way leads on to way."

"Robert Frost?" I asked.

"The Road Not Taken." He was right when he said

way leads to way and you rarely ever go back down the other road if you get too comfortable on the one you're travelling. You need not even like the road; it's just the comfort, the settling in.

I opened my mouth to tell him I would not be like that, but I couldn't manage it. I should have been pounding the streets everyday, but I wasn't.

"I'll tell you what," Ralph said. "You could stay at this job and you might get better, but you might not, and the boss has already been pretty patient with you so that won't last much longer. I know a guy who knows a guy and I can get you an office job, but not the kind you want. This buddy of mine has a cleaning company and they clean office buildings after hours from about 6:00 in the evening to 3:00 or so in the morning. Not the best for a social life but good for dropping off résumés. And the buildings are the big air-conditioned ones. How does that sound?"

That sounded great. Air-conditioning. I'd spent thousands of dollars on a degree so I could be a cleaner. My parents would be so proud. Another road to go down, another road to hope I did not get too comfortable on.

The Rock

Dear Mom and Dad,

How are things with you? I finally got to see Jennifer and Kim. Karen and I got together with them and Pansy at a little Newfoundland club and had a couple of drinks. It was nice and quiet and we all had a good laugh. Nothing like old friends getting together.

Work is good. Still love the job. My boss told me I was doing a real good job the other day after I made up a new system for inventory. He said I might get a bonus for that. The name is Windmere, Mom, not Windy Mores, like you said in your last letter. I do not even know what Windy Mores would mean. Windmere is the last name of the owner, Charles Windmere. Anyway, I am doing excellent. It is better than I ever expected. Karen is good and says hi. Give Taylor a kiss for me.

Love, Lisa

Between their work, my work and the fact that we lived at opposite ends of the city, I was in Toronto for over four weeks before I saw Jennifer and Kim. I talked to them on the phone, but our schedules were never right to get together. Now finally, we had plans for Friday night and I could not wait to catch up, vent about Rain, Dreg and the cubby-hole and get pie-eyed.

I had another week left to punch at Windmere before I started my new job at Aardvark Cleaners. I didn't believe Ralph when he first told me the name of the company, since it was one of the stupidest names I'd ever heard, but then he explained that the owner wanted to ensure he would be the first cleaner in the yellow pages. Sad, really that he went through all that trouble to incorporate the company with that stupid name before he checked it out and discovered that AAA cleaners was before him. Anyway, so I was going to start my new job soon and was about to leave the hot factory floor. That in itself was reason enough to celebrate with the girls.

Jennifer and Kim had also invited Pansy, from Fogo, to join us. Pansy was Kim's roommate in Squires House, the residence we lived in at Memorial University, or MUN, as we called it. Pansy seemed quite the snob when she first moved into the residence. She wouldn't speak to any of us and always kept to herself. Jennifer, never the one to be quiet if she didn't like a situation, called her a stuck-up bitch after a lobby party one night. This caused Pansy to cry and bawl while explaining that her mother had died the year before of breast cancer. To say the least, Jennifer felt bad. She did everything for Pansy for weeks afterwards, and so did most of the rest of the girls at Squires who were told what Pansy had been going through.

So the four of us–me, Pansy, Jennifer and Kim–were going to get together for a good old reunion. Pansy was staying with her aunt in Mississauga and the plan was that she and I would stay at Kim and Jennifer's that night. They had a one bedroom apartment in which they shared the bed and Jennifer's cousin Billy was sleeping on their couch while he looked for work. I was looking forward to meeting them at the bar I had been hearing about since Kim and Jennifer first landed in Toronto: The Rock.

The Rock was a Newfoundland bar that mixed a smattering of traditional Newfoundland music with lots of pop and rock music. There was even a little disco left over. A big, burly guy from Burin, named Jack Mullet, ran it. Jack loved parties and music, but most of all he loved Newfoundland.

The girls had told me about the place in the many letters we exchanged since they left home. They had also told me about their numerous adventures there: the guy who told them he needed to screw a Newfie to win a bet and the drinks which made their way over his head; the woman who came to the club and asked Jennifer and Kim how they had learned English so well-Jennifer gave her some words she won't soon forget, mostly of the four letter variety. At the Rock, they had met lots of guys and some wonderful new friends, but the club's main attraction was that it offered the best, the absolute best, partying. I couldn't wait to see my friends or the club and to have a Rain-free night of normality. At least, that was the plan.

I mentioned where I was going to Rain that afternoon and she had an odd reaction. It looked like a mixture of hurt because I hadn't invited her and disgust at me for going to such a clichéd, cookie-cutter Newfoundland club.

"That's fine, I guess, if you want to go to that type of club with your friends," she said. The word 'friends' was spat out like she had said the word 'murderers.' "I wouldn't have gone even if you asked which you didn't."

"Oh, I'm sorry. I just didn't think you would want to go," I said in all honesty. "I figured it wasn't your scene."

"Well, it's not, but I could have been asked," she answered.

She was pulling on her nose ring–a habit I hated. What is the difference between that and picking your nose? It's just as gross and more painful looking. She didn't have a nice little stud; it was a nose ring, a large hoop she would occasionally hook to a chain which then hooked to an equally big earring. Wouldn't take much for a mugger to rob her. He could just grab the chain and threaten to pull if she didn't cough up the goods. The thought gave me the willies, but there was many the time that I was tempted to pull that chain myself.

"Honest, I'm sorry. I didn't think you would want to go. Please, come with us if you want. I'm sure the girls would love to see you."

I was lying through my teeth. I was pretty sure the girls would be horrified to see her and even more horrified once they'd been with her for a while. I found myself torn between not wanting her to go, since if she went it would mean a dark cloud of rain hanging over us all evening, and wanting her to go so I could be entertained by the disgust of my old friends over the new and improved Karen.

The girls had told me in their letters that they had called Karen a couple of times but had never gotten together with her. They said she seemed snobbish and only talked about the arts, but I think that had been pre-Dreg. I think Karen had been artsy and a little different before Dreg but he really sent her over the edge–she was tumbling rapidly into plain weirdness. My friends had no idea what she was like now.

"Okay," Rain shocked me by saying. "I'll go with you but I might not stay long. If it's a lot of accordion and fiddle music I won't stand it. I can't take that stereotypical crap." She sneered and rolled her eyes as she spoke, which made for a very unattractive face.

"Okay, sure," I said. Well, if nothing else I figured it would make the evening interesting. "I was planning to stay over at Kim and Jennifer's anyway so you can leave whenever you want."

"Perhaps you would rather if I leave before I get there. Don't sound so happy that I might not stick around for long."

I'm pretty sure that were I to have literally bit my

tongue as hard as I did figuratively at that moment, blood loss would have been massive and transfusions would have been required. But I said nothing. I would not beg her to go. I just went into the bathroom and closed the door. The only privacy I ever got was in the bathroom.

Two hours later, I was getting my clothes out of the footlocker and was just about to change when Rain emerged from her bedroom. Apparently, the Rain I had seen for the past few weeks was less bizarre than she could be. As I looked at her the evening flashed before me–incredulous looks from strangers and shocked looks from my old friends.

She stood with her legs wide apart in a fighting stance, staring at me with a defiant look. She had a bigger nose ring than I had ever seen. It was a huge silver hoop joined by that chain to a smaller hoop in her eyebrow. Her ring of fuzz was slicked with some kind of grease that made it look more sparse than usual. She had on extra black eyeliner that made her pale skin look paler. She was decked out in a black T-shirt, black tights and a long black, flared skirt that hung down to her black hiking boots.

But the pink stripe in the middle of her little ring of head fuzz really set the look off.

"Still want me to go with you?" she asked.

I nodded, unable to say anything. What could I say?

"Well, you better get ready," she said and plopped down on the couch with her legs apart. "Can't wait to see the girls."

I think the only reason she wanted to go was to shock

Kim, Jennifer and Pansy. I'm not sure why. At some point, she had decided to rebel against society and now she wanted to flaunt it as extremely as she could. Boy did it ever work.

We could hear the music outside the door of the Rock. The building looked like a warehouse with a big map of Newfoundland on it. Joan Jett and the Blackhearts were singing my favourite song, "I Love Rock and Roll." Rain sneered and muttered that this was even worse than accordion music. I opened the door and would have felt so happy and cool had I not had the freak show next to me. One by one every head turned toward us. I don't suppose anyone looking like that had ever walked into the Rock before.

I heard two guys yell "freak" before I saw Jennifer wave us over. I use the term 'wave' loosely. She raised her hand to mouth level then moved it slightly, sort of like a royal wave. I think she was probably deciding if she should let us know where they were sitting or hide in the corner. Regardless, by the time we got over to their table the girls were hugging me and squealing with delight. Rain just stood there.

"Oh," I said, "look, here is Karen. You remember Karen."

I could see them trying to see her in there amongst the gloom, trying to find a hint of the girl they had once known so well. They each smiled faintly and said hi before Rain started in. I wished I could have warned them about her, but she was always there when I spoke to them on the phone so I had hardly mentioned her or the boyfriend.

"It is Rain, not Karen," she said. "Why can't you get that right?"

A guy walked up to us who had obviously passed one too many about three beers back. I should say that he staggered up to us on cowboy boots that his jeans were tucked into. He then got right in Rain's face and looked her over for a second.

"And where are you from, my dear?" he asked, swaying as he spoke. I could smell stale beer on his breath so I could only imagine how it smelled to Rain.

I knew Rain's get-up was obviously a means of getting attention. I'm not exactly sure why she wanted the attention but there was no doubt that blending in or keeping a low profile was not on her agenda. Still, there's attention grabbing and then there's creating a disturbance which is what Rain did in response to Beer Breath's question. She let out a loud, blood-curdling scream. The few people who had not yet noticed her turned with everyone else to focus their full attention on the woman in black. Beer Breath took a step back when he was midway through a particularly wide sway, which landed him on his ass. Unable to balance himself any better on his ass than his legs, back he went.

"Leave me alone, asshole," Rain yelled to him as he lay on the floor. She stepped over him, walked to an empty seat at Pansy's table and plopped herself down.

"That's Karen?" Kim asked. "What happened to her?"

"I can hear you," Rain said loudly.

"Well, you do look really different, Karen," Jennifer said. Pansy nodded and looked from Jennifer to me to Karen.

Their reactions to Rain were perfect snapshots of these three people. Kim, with her short brown hair, dimpled chin and extra 20 or 30 pounds, loved to talk, especially about others, but was never confrontational. Blond haired, blue-eyed Jennifer would speak her mind and face down the devil without batting an eye. She was confident and believed in herself more than anyone I have ever known. Then there was Pansy, the follower. Pansy's long brown hair framed a long narrow face with beautiful deep green eyes. Where Jennifer had confidence, Pansy had none. She followed and never led, nodded and agreed with whomever was speaking, never developing an opinion of her own. She was only in Toronto because she followed Jennifer and Kim after they moved up there. They helped her get a job at the same accounting firm Jennifer worked at.

So, in perfect form, Jennifer was confrontational with Rain, Kim had only spoken about her and not to her and Pansy had nodded. It was like pieces of a puzzle fitting together as I watched them reacting.

"It is Rain," she spoke up, "and yes, I have changed. I'm not going to stay the same as I was in high school. I wouldn't want to stay the same."

"Well, if being different is what you're going for then you've done it very well," Jennifer said then sat down three chairs away from Rain.

There were only four chairs at the table because they had not been expecting Rain. "I can stand," Pansy said, "I'm okay."

Jennifer tutted and walked over to another table where they seemed to have an abundance of chairs and spoke to someone sitting there. She picked up a chair and plopped it next to Pansy at the corner of the table.

"Okay, what is everyone drinking?" I asked once everyone was seated. I could not really afford a round but felt bad for bringing Rain to our parade and wanted to make up for it. "Labatt Blue?"

All parties nodded except for Rain. "I'll have a pint of Guinness," she said. "No bottled beer for me."

"Oh, for Christ's sake, have a bottle of beer," Jennifer said loudly over the sound of the Pretenders singing about being on a chain gang.

"I would like a pint of Guinness, please. Bottled beer tastes watery and I don't think it should matter to anyone else what I drink."

"So, you'd rather chew your beer, would you?" Jennifer asked.

"Give me a hand. Jennifer," I said. I wanted to get her away from Rain before they came to blows.

I shook my head as Jennifer and I walked to the bar. "Sorry, but she made me feel like dirt for not inviting her so I asked her to come. At least you don't have to live with her."

"She's crazy. I never seen nothing like that before in my life," Jennifer said, proving why she had failed English 1000 in university the first time she tried. "Why stay with her? Maybe we could get a bigger apartment and you could move in or maybe Pansy would leave her aunt's."

"I'll move in with a stranger first," I said. "I'll never live with either one of ye again. We're definitely better friends than roommates."

Jennifer laughed. No one could deny that when the four of us rented an apartment on Higgins Line in St. John's, the results were less than perfect. Boyfriends and money had led from bickering to an actual fistfight between Jennifer and me. I moved out and Jennifer was not far behind. You never know people until you live with them and I have no doubt that our friendship would have ended if we had lived together any longer. Jennifer and I patched things up once we had distance and separate addresses between us.

"You're right, I know but that," she pointed to Rain, "can't be any good either."

"I'm saving and then, if I can find someone to share a place with, I'm getting the Hell out of there. You have no idea. You haven't even met Dreg."

"Dreg? What's that if you were going to write home about it?"

Jennifer took the four bottles of beer while I paid. I watched the bartender slop Guinness all over the bar as he passed it to me. It was filled to the brim and I knew I would have a hard time getting back to the table without getting any on me.

"Rain's boyfriend. He's a musician and an arsehole. They're both so weird and all they seem to do is have sex."

"Ewww," Jennifer said then laughed again. I wanted to hug her. It was so good to see her and feel connected again.

I heard Kim and Pansy laughing long before I got to the table. Rain looked disgusted and was repeatedly telling them to shut up.

"So how do you like Dreg?" Pansy asked emphasis on the word Dreg.

I put the Guinness down in front of Rain, flicked the extra liquid off my hands and shrugged. Like mother told me, "If I don't have anything good to say, don't say anything." Okay, so I haven't always been known to abide by that rule, but I wasn't about to set Rain off any more than she already seemed to be and I honestly couldn't think of one good thing to say.

"That's a foolish name, though isn't it, Lisa?" Kim said. She was laughing so hard, tears streamed down her face.

And then it happened. It seemed like it was in slow motion as Rain threw her pint in Kim's face. Now a pint is not a small amount. If you throw it, it's bound to hit people close to the intended target. In this case, that meant Pansy and a not quite seated Jennifer.

"Jesus." "Bitch." "Stupid." "Slut." Words were flying all over the place and Rain was out the door before anyone noticed her leave the table. She might have wanted the drama of throwing the drink at someone but she was not stupid enough to stick around for the aftermath. I'm sure someone, namely Jennifer, would have smacked Rain if she had stuck around. As it was, Kim was soaked and could not stay. Jennifer and Pansy were also wet and I hadn't been spared. We all stunk of beer.

Our night at the Rock was over so we all went to Jennifer's where we took turns showering and changed into pyjamas and drank the boring bottled beer we bought on the way. We may have left the Rock but I had a ball talking and drinking all night with the girls. Rain missed a good time but we did not miss Rain.

None of us were very good friends with her after that, but we would be there for her if she needed us, just like any old friends would. Weird that the person we liked the least would be the one who ended up needing us the most.

The Ugly Side of Love

Dear Mom and Dad,

How are you guys? I hope all is well with you. Everything is good here now. Karen's mom and dad are staying with me and Karen is well. Sorry about getting upset on the phone. Everything is fine, really. I will write you more later and catch you up when things are settled down a little more. I am doing really well and so is Karen. I was just a little freaked out when I was talking to you. Please don't worry. Give Taylor a kiss for me.

Love, Lisa

I should have seen it; I must have seen it. I should have paid more attention to the scattered bruise on her forearm or that swollen lip she told me was from an infection in her lip stud. Or the time she wore a turtleneck and I saw that her neck was covered in what I said were bruises, but she insisted were hickeys. I should have seen it. I didn't. I denied it. I lived in the same apartment and ignored the huge fights in the bedroom. I never heard a smack, but I should have seen or heard something. I was the poster girl for denial, hired by the Canadian Psychologists Association and I did my job well, too damned well.

That was until I walked into the apartment that day. I had been cleaning toilets at Aardvark–oh, yes, the new girl gets toilet duty–for six weeks and it was my day off. I remember the time exactly because I checked my watch before I went in the apartment. It was 4:13 p.m. and I thought that if I was lucky and they went to bed early, I had only six or seven hours with them until I got a little peace. I opened the door and knew, before even looking into the apartment, that something was wrong. I don't know what it was. I just knew. Maybe Rain had sent out some negative aura strong enough to smack me up side of the head, maybe it was the smell of blood and urine mixed together or maybe it was the silence–no droning, weird chants or Indian music. Regardless, my feeling was right.

I opened the door slowly to find her lying on the kitchen floor in a puddle of blood. I could see she'd wet her tan pants as they were now dark and I could smell the strong scent of urine. Her beige shirt, as bright as Rain ever wore and only then because it was part of her outfit for her latest play, was now red with blood. Her head was covered with her own sticky blood, oozing from a split on the side of her scalp. I could tell from the twisted position of her arm that it was most likely broken. On the wall were bloody fingerprints where it looked like she had tried to get to the phone.

I remember my heart felt like it stopped beating for a few seconds. Then, as if it had taken a long breath for the difficult journey ahead, it started to beat so fast I could feel the pulse in my neck. I wondered what had happened. Was the person who did this still here and would they do it to me? Was she going to be okay? These thoughts all went through my mind as I went to her, as if by instinct, and checked her pulse. Hers was so very weak and I wished I could share mine with her since it seemed to be going at super speed.

I'd left the door open and now I screamed for help. No one came. I reached up, got the phone and dialled 911. I smeared blood all over the phone as I screamed at the operator that my friend was hurt and needed help; her pulse was weak. No, I didn't know who did it. Could they please come soon? No, I didn't know what had happened; I'd just gotten home and found her this way. Yes, I wanted the police to come. No, I hadn't checked the rest of the apartment. She was bleeding from the head and seemed to have a broken arm. No, I didn't know who had done it. Why did they keep asking that?

Before I knew it, the police and an ambulance arrived almost simultaneously. The ambulance driver said I could go to the hospital with her. The police suggested I stay there to answer some questions. I thought about her waking up in the ambulance, afraid and with a stranger,so I asked the cops if they could question me later. The superintendent was there by then and I figured he could look after them. Rain was coming first now and to Hell with anyone else.

The officers asked me if there was someone else they needed to get in touch with. I remembered Dreg and suddenly felt even sicker to my stomach. *My God*, I thought, *he couldn't have done this, could he?* The things I'd noticed previously but ignored now came to my mind and I felt horrible. This couldn't be right. No way would he have done this. It didn't make sense; like the fact that my roommate had her head bashed in and was being rushed to the hospital made sense. I told the officer my fears about Dreg and they agreed to track him down.

A half an hour later, I was sitting in the hospital waiting for Jennifer to come by. When I'd called her, she said she'd bring me a change of clothes and some moral support. Shortly after getting to the hospital, I'd started shaking and still hadn't stopped. A kind nurse told me she could see if a doctor would give me something to calm me down, but I refused. I wanted to be alert if Rain needed me. Damn, I felt terrible for thinking all those bad things about her. She'd looked so sad and horrible on the floor. What had she gone through before she was knocked out? I couldn't even imagine.

Jennifer came into the emergency room and I surprised myself by breaking down, sobbing in her arms when she hugged me. I suddenly felt weak so she helped me to a chair. I don't know how long I was there, crying like a little baby, but the next thing I knew the doctor was asking who was with Karen Keane. I looked up, afraid to say it was me since I wasn't sure I wanted to hear what he had to say.

"We're here with her," I said as I motioned to Jennifer then pointed to myself.

"I'm Doctor Ramaz," the doctor said. He had a heavy East Indian accent. "Miss Keane's head injury is severe, I'm afraid. There was considerable haemorrhaging. The next twenty-four hours will be critical. She also has multiple contusions around her neck, a broken arm and a broken jaw. She's lucky to be alive. It's a good thing you got there when you did."

He looked down at the floor, as if searching for the right thing to say. "Her condition is critical," he said, as he gently put his hand on mine. I was surprised and touched by the gesture. It felt comfortable there, not threatening or patronizing. "If there are others to call–her family–it would be best to do that now."

His eyes said it all. He thought Rain was going to die. Everybody back home better join us in Hell now or they would never see her alive again. Once again, my tears overwhelmed me.

I would have to tell Rain's mother, Brenda, who seemed as confused and frustrated with the changes in her daughter as I was. I would answer the phone sometimes when she called. She seemed happy to talk to me, said I seemed cheerier than Karen was. She still called her Karen. She told me that she'd named her Karen and christened her Karen and that was her name. She always sounded so sad, so disappointed that Rain had turned out the way she did. Not that she wasn't proud of her in some ways, she was. Rain was a successful performer and Brenda would beam with pride when she talked to my mom about Rain's acting. She just seemed sad for the same reasons I did. Sad because we couldn't talk to her the way we used to, couldn't go to the mall with her or gossip with her. I sometimes got the feeling Brenda was envious of my relationship with my mom. I always talked a lot to Brenda when she called, always tried to speak with her the way Rain would have if she had stayed Karen.

Brenda and I had grown closer and now I had to break her heart. No, I was going to rip her heart out of her chest, hold it up to her face and say, "here's your heart." I was going to change her world in the way mine had been changed. We would never be the same again. Violence had touched us, smashed us and we couldn't live in ignorant denial of it any more. It didn't just happen to other people.

I remember going into the little family room the doctor brought me to. I was going to call directory assistance since I no longer remembered Rain's number in Carmanville. I called Mom. She could look it up, I thought. It was selfish maybe to call her first, but it made sense at the time, more so when Mom picked up the phone and I started to bawl. Sometimes, even thousands of miles away, a girl just needs to cry to her mom. She listened and comforted, horrified at what had happened–she'd say a prayer for Karen. She gave me Brenda's number after offering to call for me. No, I told her, this was something I had to do myself. It wasn't fair to Brenda, or my mom, to pawn it off.

My hands shook as I dialled the number. I waited as three rings went in, each one feeling like there were minutes in between. She answered the phone with a cheery hello. I wondered what she had been doing the minute before I crashed the world down around her. Had she been baking some of her wonderful chocolate chip cookies or knitting, maybe quietly reading a book, secure in the sanity of the world? How quickly things can change for us, any of us, at any one moment. Every one of us could have received such a call or visit. Each of us might learn what it means to go from safety to chaos, all in the blink of an eye.

"Brenda?" I said, my voice quivering. "Is Ron there?" It just came out. It was what we did. Talk to the father; to the man. When I had a car accident a few years before, I called from the hospital asking for my dad. Mom always asked what was wrong when I asked for Dad.

"No?" she said; a question in her voice. Who was this young girl calling her husband? "Who's speaking?"

"It's Lisa," I answered.

There was a pause. She knew and I knew she knew. I would only call and ask for Ron if something was wrong. I heard her breath quicken and wished to God I was not in that damned family room so far away. I wanted to hug her and reassure her. I wanted to help her find this out slowly, easily somehow. I closed my eyes as I fought back new tears at the thought of her there alone and asked God to help me find the right words. I'd asked God for that before on a couple of occasions and, I must say, it worked. Poor God. I was asking for an easy way to tell a woman that her daughter had been beaten almost to death and that she should get her butt up here now if she wanted to see her alive again. Sometimes we ask so much of God.

"What is it?" she asked breathlessly. There was no need for formalities. We both knew this wasn't a social call.

"It's Rain, ah, Karen," I said, stating the obvious.

"Oh God, what happened?"

"She's in the hospital. She's okay," I lied. "But I think it would be good for you to come up, as soon as you can. Ron too, and Johnny and Ben. Her family."

Strength came through in her voice that I'd heard from people before, mostly women, when they reach down deep for courage and hold off the tears and pain long enough to deal with the issue at hand.

"How is she? Really."

"Not good," I said reluctantly. "The doctor said the family should get here soon," I said, realizing that the truth was the only thing left to say. There was no cushioning it and even if I did, Brenda would know.

"Okay," she said in a monotone voice.

"I'll pick you up at the airport," I helped her get her plan in action. "I'll call you back in half an hour and you, or whoever is there, can tell me what flight you're on and when I can pick you up." I wondered as I said it where they would get the money. Ron only had a seasonal job with the Department of Highways in the winter. Brenda sold a few crafts. They didn't have much.

"Was it an accident?" she asked.

"I found her lying on the floor at home. I'll explain it when you get here."

"Oh," she said; relief in her voice. I guess it made her feel better that Rain was at home and not out in the street somewhere when it happened. Funny how our ideas of what's safe and what's not changes depending on our circumstance.

"Is there anything else I can do for you?" I asked. "Can I call someone?"

"Stay with her, would you?"

"I will."

"Thank you. As long as there is someone there she loves. Oh, is Dreg there?" she asked, his name catching in her throat.

"No, I don't know where he is."

"Oh." Silence. Seconds passed. "I'll be there as soon as I can. Thank you. Karen is lucky to have a friend like you. Goodbye."

"Goodbye," I said. I hung up the phone feeling guilty. Was she lucky to have me? I should have seen this coming. Maybe I could have prevented it. Like Rain would listen to me. Maybe this wasn't even what I thought it was.

Jennifer opened the door and the look on her face told me something was wrong.

"What?"

"She took a turn for the worse. Her heart stopped. The doctor said they resuscitated her, but it's very touch and go."

"I can't believe this. It's a dream, isn't it?"

Jennifer shook her head and held my hand.

Three hours later, I was biding my time in the waiting room when Dreg came in. He was handcuffed and accompanied by two of the cops that had been at our place earlier. Dreg looked at me then at the floor. I knew then, in that one look, that he had done this. I wondered if he felt guilty. One of the cops went to the front desk with Dreg while the other, spotting me, came over.

"Why is he here?" I asked, indignant at the thought that he may have wanted to see her.

"He has some scratches on his neck. They need to be treated and photographed. They'll have to take evidence from your friend's fingernails to see if it was her that scratched him."

"Oh, he was probably scratched by someone else he beat the shit out of today," I said.

"He needs to get his hand x-rayed too," the officer said, ignoring my remark. "Seems he may have broken it somehow." He looked me in the eye and I saw an anger that surprised me considering that he probably saw this kind of thing every day.

"So, why don't you let him suffer?"

"We can't. We have to make sure he's looked after medically."

"Don't you hate that?" I asked. "Don't you fucking hate that?"

He nodded his head. "We have to make sure that when this goes to trial he can't whine about us not looking after his rights."

I said nothing. I started to walk toward the desk where Dreg stood. The officer next to me grabbed my arm lightly.

"Take your hand off me," I said with a rage I never knew I had in me. "I'm going to the desk to ask about my friend and I don't think you can stop me."

"Don't touch him," he said as he let go of my arm. "If you do, I'll have to take you in."

"That will break your heart," I said. I sounded mean and would regret it later. He couldn't have liked what he was doing.

I marched up to Dreg, ignoring the alarmed look on the face of the cop next to him. Pointing my finger as close to his face as I felt comfortable with, I started to rhyme off enough expletives to shock a sailor. Dreg just kept staring at me.

"Don't think you'll get away with this," I shouted as the cop I'd been talking to previously stepped in front of me. "If she dies I'll make sure you rot in jail. I'll testify against you."

"There's nothing to testify about," Dreg said flatly. "I

never did anything to her. She won't testify against me."

"That's not an option if she dies, is it? Are you fucking happy that she might die? Is that what you wanted when you were hitting her and she was scratching you and trying to protect herself? Was it?" Jesus, I was madder than I'd ever been before. If the cops had left me alone I swear I would have killed him. I didn't think that was possible before, but ever since that moment, I know that capacity rests inside me somewhere and it scares me.

He shook his head. "How is she?" he asked. He seemed genuinely concerned and I found it hard to comprehend.

"She's barely alive," I said. "Her family has been called in. That's how she is. You better hope to Jesus that you're behind bars when they get here because her father could kill you with one hand and he'll be angry enough to do it."

Ron Keane was a big, strapping man. Not fat, all muscle with the biggest hands I'd ever seen. He was rough without intending to be so and reminded me of my grandfather.

Dreg just looked at me as a nurse called out, "Richard Carlisle."

"Come on," the officer said, grabbing Dreg by the shirt and pulling him toward the nurse.

"Richard? That's your name? I always knew you were a dick," I yelled after him as he was being pulled away.

Nine hours later I was at Toronto Airport waiting for those sad people to come off the plane. I'd gotten to see Rain before I left and they were in for a horrible shock. Tubes stuck out of her everywhere. Her head was completely shaved because of the stitches all over it. Her parents hadn't seen Rain's latest hairstyles so this would be a surprise. Rain's arm was in a cast and her face was a mass of bruises. It was going to hurt them deeply to see their loved one like that.

They stepped out of the gate looking more tired and scared than anyone deserved to be. The six of them–Rain's mother, father, two brothers, sister-in-law and grandmother–dragged themselves through the airport. There were faint smiles when they recognized me, more for my benefit than theirs, I think. But, then again, maybe they were genuinely happy to see a familiar face in this big, lonely place full of strangers.

"Is she..." Brenda stopped without finishing her question.

"She's the same," I reassured her, relief showing in her face. Her daughter was still alive and she would see her one more time. A sad thing to be happy about.

"What happened?" Ron asked quickly. "Did she have an aneurysm or something?"

An aneurysm? I'd told them she was found in her apartment. It was a logical conclusion, I guess. A non-violent, sudden aneurysm. That thought probably sustained them all the way here. Now, once again, Lisa the Destroyer was going to burst their bubble. I was going to have to tell them the gruesome, unbelievable truth.

"No, there was no aneurysm." I delayed the inevitable.

"What then?" Ron insisted.

"It was Dreg," I said, not knowing how to put it. "He hit her." I was the master of understatement.

I will never forget the looks on their faces, especially Ron's. There is something within a father that feels he should protect his daughter for life, and anything that happens to her is his fault. Their faces reflected disbelief and pain. Someone had hurt their loved one; someone she loved had intentionally hurt her.

"He put her in the hospital?" Ron asked emphasis on hospital.

I nodded, trying to put the thought of Rain lying there in her own blood, out of my head.

"Then he hurt her bad?" Rain's brother, Ben asked.

"Yes," I whispered. "I'm sorry. It was pretty bad. I found her. Let's pick up your bags and I'll tell you about it on the way to the hospital." I wanted to wait, to tell them all of the horrible details in a private place. They didn't need to hear of their Karen's battering in the middle of this impersonal place.

I'd borrowed a van from Frank, a guy from home. I hardly had to ask. He, like most everyone from home, would give you the shirt off his back if you needed it. I had started to tell him about what happened and, before I finished my story, he offered to drive me. I opted to do it myself. Jennifer was still at the hospital in case Rain needed anything. I didn't know how to get in touch with any of Rain's friends, at least not until I could get back to the apartment and her address book.

On the way to the hospital I told them, breaking down a couple of times, despite my best efforts. I didn't want them to think it was that bad, bad enough to make me cry. Fact of the matter was that they would find out when they saw her. So, I stopped trying to shelter them and told them the truth. I prepared them for how bad she looked. Ron clenched his fists. I wished I could get Dreg away from the cops for a little meeting with him and his two sons.

At the hospital, I walked them to her room and watched them crumble, one by one, as they saw her battered, broken body in the bed. When Ron cried, it ripped my heart out. God, how I hated to see a guy cry. Brenda stayed there as long as the nurses would let her, holding her daughter's hand and crying, praying as Ron cursed the ground Dreg walked on. It was surreal then and like a dream now, in retrospect.

I went back to the cubby-hole early the next morning, called in sick to work (the second time in two weeks; I hated cleaning toilets) and packed a few things to take to Jennifer's. This was a crime scene and one didn't sleep in a crime scene. Besides, I was afraid. For all I knew, Dreg would be out on bail or some such legal shit and come back there. I wondered if he would he hit someone who didn't care for him.

I was just about to leave the apartment, suitcases packed, when there was a knock on the door. My heart raced as I looked out the peephole and saw Ron. I opened the door and wondered how he'd gotten there.

"Ron?" I said.

He stood there, looking past me as his face paled. I turned to see what he was looking at: the blood on the floor; her bloody handprints on the wall; and her blood, from my hands, on the phone. The cops had told me not to clean it until the scene was cleared.

"Ron, I'm sorry," I said, apologizing for something I had no control over. He shouldn't have had to see that.

"How?" he said in a voice barely audible. "How did this happen? Did he hit her before? Why didn't you do anything about it? You could have told me. I would have come up to kill the son of a bitch myself. Her blood shouldn't be there. She shouldn't be in that goddamn hospital bed."

His voice rose with every word. I was startled, but knew he needed to get it off his chest. And so, I abided. He swore some more then started to cry. I held him as he sobbed on my shoulder. This man, who had been another father to me, now leaned on me. I felt humbled at his shameless ability to let it go. I took him into the living room, my bedroom, and sat him down on the sofa. I sat on the footlocker.

He had questions and I wanted to answer them. I went to the kitchen again, trying to ignore the blood and grabbed my friend, the Captain, as in Captain Morgan dark rum. I had no mix. Just as well. Pouring up two stiff drinks, I asked God to help me find the right words.

Ron took the drink from me without a word. I sat down on the locker again and took a long drink. My eyes watered as the liquor stung my throat.

"I don't think I saw it before," I said, looking him in the eyes. "In hindsight, I guess there were signs but they certainly weren't obvious. I never saw or heard him hit her. They argued a lot, mostly him shouting at her. I thought she was so independent but this guy seemed to have a spell on her. He's a jerk. That's obvious now but he was always such a…a," what the Hell, I was 22 years old and we were sitting in a bloody apartment drinking Captain Morgan. Why pull punches? "A prick," I said. "She thought he was great. He was a musician, smart; a writer of dark lyrics. I'd point out that he didn't treat her very well but that would only make her mad." I looked down. "Most everything I said seemed to make her mad. We are very different now."

He nodded as he listened. "I know what you mean. It's been difficult to connect with her. Brenda finds it really hard. We love her so much though."

"I know. Me too." And I did. I hadn't realized it until this happened; our roots of friendship held me firm to her. I may not have always liked her, but I still loved her, no matter what.

He sighed. "How are you doing? This must have been a Hell of a shock for you too."

I nodded, fighting back the tears. It was still so fresh in my mind and it touched me that he could consider how I felt during his time of need.

We sat there for another five minutes. Neither of us spoke. We both seemed comfortable with the silence. Finally, he said he should get back to the hospital. I asked him how he got to the apartment. He told me he'd taken a cab. I offered to drive him back to the hospital as I still had the van. As we were leaving, the phone rang. I wasn't going to answer it but something told me I should.

"Hurry to the hospital," Ben's voice said.

"What is it?" I asked.

"Hurry," he said. "Just get here." The dial tone sounded loud in my ear as I turned to Ron.

The Ugly Side of Love Too

Dear Mom and Dad,

How is everything with you? Karen is doing really well now. Her mom and dad are gone back home and we are back in our apartment, enjoying being home. Things are getting back to normal. It is almost as if it never happened. She still has not heard from her old boyfriend since he got out of jail. He never showed his face around here and I am glad of that.

Work is still good. Windmere Packaging just received a business award and my boss told me I was a big part of them getting it. He said that I was an efficiency expert. Pretty good, hey?

I went to a hockey game last night. It was unbelievable. Toronto won 10 8. 18 goals! And five of them were in under two minutes. That has to be some kind of record. I thought of you the whole time, Dad. You would have loved it.

We'll have to go to a game if you ever get up here for a visit. Don't worry, Mom, we won't make you go.

Anyway, that is all here. Give Taylor a treat for me and rub her little head.

Love, Lisa

Rain had awakened from her coma. The doctor said she was out of the woods. Little did we know that this was just the beginning. Rain claimed she couldn't remember what happened. She couldn't testify against Dreg because she couldn't remember. The cops said that without her testimony, they couldn't do a thing. We all tried to talk sense into her, but the more we tried the more angry and defensive of Dreg she became. It was like watching a movie where one of the characters is going down into a dark cellar to investigate the creepy noises coming from there and you want to scream at her. Only we could talk to the character and she could hear us, but she wouldn't listen.

I knew she remembered what Dreg had done. I saw it in the flicker of fear in her eyes the first time she saw him in the hospital room after he got out on bail. Now that was interesting. Imagine Mr. Dreg strolling into a room full of people who wanted to rip his scalp off. The tension was palpable. Dreg seemed oblivious of it at first. Then suddenly, he seemed to become aware of it and said he would be back in a few minutes. He didn't return until the next day.

Rain was not there when Dreg arrived. She had gone to get her arm x-rayed. Ron, Ben, Jimmy and I were having a game of Five Hundreds while Grandma Keane and Brenda watched. Dreg walked into the room, saw no sign of Rain and turned to leave until Ron stood in front of him. A chill goes up my spine as I remember this because words had never scared me like that before or since. He was angry, spitting angry.

"Listen you," he said, eerily calm. "You may legally be able to walk in here and you may legally be able to come near my daughter. But I'm a moral man and the moral law is in effect here. Oh, we're all quiet, stunned Newfies to you, lost in this big city and you're the man with all the contacts. You're safe, right? You sleep at night, secure that you'll have a peaceful rest." Ron stepped a little closer to Dreg and pointed his finger at him. The look on his face made my blood run cold. I think it had the same effect on Dreg because he didn't say a word.

"But you remember this, Mister," he continued, his voice even softer. "You remember this because one night you'll be sleeping, dreaming of whatever shit you dream of, and you'll wake up to the feel of cold steel on your neck. I know that feeling. See the scar?" he asked as he pulled down the collar of his white dress shirt he'd worn for two of the last four days. The scar was from an accident at a fish plant with a gutting knife.

"When it cuts into your skin, you feel pain first, then you feel the cold of the blade and the warmth of the blood. It will be slow and I'll make sure you feel every bit of it because I can. I've gutted fish, skinned moose and I've bled them too, slit their throats to do it. It had to be done that way. Some things a man has to do for his family. To tell you the truth, I usually felt guilty about the moose, felt a little bad for having to do it. I won't feel guilty about pulling that knife across your throat." His voice was so cool and every word sounded like gospel. "I'll smile when I do it." He smiled. I'm not sure if it was for effect or not, but it did the trick. "Some things a man has to do for his family."

Ron stopped talking and just stared at Dreg, not blinking. His sons stepped behind him, towered behind him, each of them taller than Ron by at least five inches. Dreg looked at them all and walked out. He didn't even swallow. His mouth must have been as dry as mine, drier since I only heard the words. They weren't directed at me.

We never said a word to Rain, or to anyone else that Dreg had been there. I don't know if Dreg ever told her. I don't think so. He would have sounded whiny if he told tales on her dad. Besides, I wouldn't think he would want to remember it enough to tell her about it. I saw the look of abject fear on Dreg's face that day, and I'm pretty sure he would never admit to it.

I know it sounds incredible but he left after that and

went back to Alberta. He didn't stick around to control her some more, he just left. Ron Keane from Carmanville had frightened the shit out of him. I guess Dreg figured his options were limited in Toronto for a while.

Poor Rain was devastated. She'd been beaten half to death, more than three quarters to death if the truth be told, and she'd stood by her man. Seemingly, at least to her, he had left her for no reason. She'd defended him and he'd abandoned her. There were times I wanted to tell her that Dreg had been run out of town, that her father had made our blood run cold with his threats and Dreg was too big a coward to deal with someone closer to his own size. I knew if I said anything, Rain would never forgive her father so I shut up for once in my life. I couldn't help her lose the one man in her life who loved her, and who always would. I have to admit I loved Ron too. I loved what he had said and that he never flinched while looking in the face of evil. I knew that if I ever needed something and my dad wasn't around, I'd feel safe going to Ron.

Rain and I went back to the cubby-hole after she got out of hospital. The first night, she offered me the bed and said she would sleep on the couch. Maybe she didn't want to be alone or maybe the bed reminded her of Dreg. After I offered to share the bed and she refused, I went in the room. The bed smelled worse than the sofa.

I heard Rain crying out in the living room and slowly, in the dark of our apartment, I crawled out to lie on the floor next to the sofa. She stopped crying when I got there so I knew she knew I was there, but she said nothing and neither did I.

Lying there on the floor, I knew I couldn't move out anytime soon. Rain was still recovering physically and I feared that the wounds I could not see would take even longer to heal. I didn't know which parts of my friend Karen would come out of this whole ugly experience. I thought maybe she would be more like she had been in high school or maybe it would push her even further over the edge of weirdness. Whatever happened, I knew I would stay with her, at least until I felt she could feel safe on her own. That's what friends do for each other, even if they don't recognize who they are anymore.

The Old Boyfriend

Dear Mom and Dad,

How are you? I am good. Work is good at Windmere. All the girls are well. We went out to a club last Friday night and ran into some old friends. It is always nice to see people from home. Sammy Hollett was there and so was Bill Cumby. You remember Bill? He was in that band, Firefight that played down to Ladle Cove Day a couple of years ago. He is going out with Helen Flynn now and she was there too. I have not seen her since high school and she has hardly changed a bit. Oh, and I saw Jimmy Whalen. He has gotten a lot fatter.

Winter is setting in firmly and there is some snow here. Only takes a bit though and the world comes to a crashing halt. It is like they close the roads and schools and businesses for flurries. They are all nish, I think. Other than that, there is not much news here. Love you both. Give Taylor a kiss for me.

Love, Lisa

Over three months after Rain was nearly killed, we finally went to the Rock again. It was still the closest thing to home in that place, and somehow I felt I could breathe again when I walked through the door. I needed it. I had just spent my first Christmas away from home and felt pretty low. The girls decided to take me out to cheer me up. The truth is that we all felt homesick around that time of year.

Rain came with us, despite her less than stellar last visit there. She was in the apartment when we were getting ready to go and, well, we just figured it was polite to ask her to come along. She hadn't gone out once since she had come home from the hospital and I still don't know why, but she said yes, which shocked and disappointed me at the same time. A wet blanket sprang to my mind and I reluctantly acted pleasantly surprised. She said she was bored enough to go out with us. I think the truth was that she didn't want to be home alone. I think as much as she wanted Dreg to walk back into her life she still feared it as well.

We drank a half dozen beer while going through the three stages of hair preparation. In stage one, we sprayed our hair with massive amounts of hairspray–I believe our combined hairdos were possibly responsible for at least half of the hole in the ozone layer. Stage two, which had to quickly follow stage one or the hairspray would dry before we completed it, was when we teased our hair straight up and then blow-dried it into position. We then waited as long as we could–drinking, gossiping and listening to songs like Michael Jackson's "Billie Jean," "Jessie's Girl" by Rick Springfield and Cyndi Lauper's "Girls Just Want to Have Fun" (play, rewind, play, rewind, play, rewind, over and over again). All this while looking like Frankenstein's brides on a bad hair day. Once it seemed we'd waited long enough (when Pansy was getting tipsy), we went to stage three and moulded the hair into position (and trust me it would stay) until we washed it or set about starting the three stages again. The final effect was a mass of hair that was high, wide and which, I feel quite strongly, could have been used as armour against any attacks on our country. Rain, of course, had no part in this hair preparation ritual.

When ready, the five of us trekked off to the club. Jennifer, Kim, Pansy and I were dressed to the nines with our hair several inches up off our heads and enough makeup to attract any man, we hoped. Rain had a new layer of black fuzz that now shrouded her whole head and covered her scar. She wore a black shirt, big black smock and matching flat black shoes. We must have looked quite the sight marching in the front door of the club: the four slutsketeers and the creature from the black lagoon. The four of us had our ears pierced twice each and Rain with her nose ring, earring, two eyebrow rings and that horrible stud in her lip. No doubt men were itching to kiss her.

We stood up at the bar, ordered our drinks–beer for us, natural spring water for Rain. There was a small scuffle when Rain didn't like the ionization of her water and argued with the bartender. Jennifer, in her ultra diplomatic way, told her to shut the fuck up or go home. Rain glared as the bartender snickered and I suddenly wished I was back in the cubby-hole.

It must have been five beers and two hours later when Jennifer asked me about Jimmy Whelan. "You remember Jimmy Whalen?" she asked me. I was sitting back on to bar, right across the table from her.

"Remember him? I still dream about him sometimes."

"Who's Jimmy Whalen," Pansy asked.

"The love of her life," Rain said with a snide, childish tone reserved for eight year olds.

Yes, I had to agree with her there. Jimmy had been the love of my life, my first love, the one who took the blossom off the tree of my girlhood and made me into a woman. Oh God, how I hate all that flowery language for describing two teenagers sweating and grunting with excitement and guilt in the back seat of a beat up old car. But I loved him. I was with him for two years, from ages 15 to 17. He gave me a promise ring, swore he loved me and I loved him deeply. I cried when he went away to university when I was barely 16 and just starting grade 11. We saw each other when he came home for vacations and I visited him twice that year in St. John's, but soon I was too young and too far away. We drifted apart and by the time I went to MUN, we were no longer together.

I saw him a few times while I was at university. Once, he was walking hand in hand down a corridor with a pretty, skinny blond and my heart ached. I ducked into a room to avoid having to talk to him while fighting the urge to cry. Another time I was at a party at Rothermere House, an all male residence, when I saw him. I was, and I have to admit I am thankful for this fact, necking up a storm with a guy in the corner when Jimmy eyed me. I looked over and noticed him staring and hoped he felt that ache as well. I waved brazenly and returned to kissing the guy I was with. God, how transparent was I?

Anyway, there I was at the Rock almost five years later and Jennifer was asking me about this blast from the past. "Why?" I asked.

She pointed, ever so discreetly toward the bar. I turned around and saw him. It was Jimmy Whalen: a little older, twenty pounds heavier and a few less hairs. He was still gorgeous, more so I think since the weight looked good on his previously skinny body. I hate it when someone says that weight looks good on somebody, since I know no one will ever say that about me. Anyway, I digress. There was Jimmy, looking so good. He was staring down at a bottle he was nursing; then swishing its contents. He was lost in thought, thank God, since I couldn't stop staring–mouth and eyes wide open. The past and the present merged and I was sure, absolutely positive, that this was fate. All these years later I had found him, standing there alone, no blond on his arm, no sweaty engineering student trying to stick his tongue down my throat. This was it.

After a moment, as if he felt someone watching him,

he looked directly at me. Somehow, I managed to close my mouth and make my eyes look just slightly wide. I smiled. A look, first of confusion then of pleasure, walked across his face. He smiled back and started to come toward me. I looked out on the floor, expecting this would be where my heart would wind up once it finally burst out of my chest. Jimmy stood there in front of me and I looked up into his beautiful, still smiling, face.

"Lisa?" he said.

"Jimmy," I answered.

His smile faded for a second then returned. "Actually, it's James now." It didn't come out sounding pompous or conceited, just a fact. He'd grown up and changed his name. I understood but, quite frankly, I was getting sick and tired of being corrected about the names of my old friends.

"James," I corrected myself.

"My God, I can't believe you're here."

I heard a loud, very loud, clearing of the throat behind me. I turned to see Pansy giving me one of her patented subtle looks. "Oh, I said. Pansy this is James, James, Pansy. You remember Jennifer Best and Kim Skinner and Karen Keane."

"Yeah, hi everybody," he said smiling. He had a confused look on his face. I'm sure he was trying to reconcile the perfect Karen to this bizarre thing in front of him.

"Actually, it's Rain now," she piped up, glaring at me for bringing up her old identity. How else was I supposed to remind him that he knew her already?

"Oh," James said.

Bonnie Tyler started to sing "Total Eclipse of the Heart."

"Dance?" James asked.

"Sure," I said. We walked out onto the dance floor. He took me in his arms and, suddenly, it felt like we were at the town hall in Ladle Cove and were dancing to Eric Clapton's "Wonderful Tonight." I closed my eyes and let myself go back in time. I realized that he smelled different. His aftershave had changed. It smelled like something fancier than the Aqua Velva he used to wear.

He must have felt the time warp too because when I put my head up to look at him, he kissed me. It was quick and gentle, a mere brush of the lips but I tingled all over and wanted more, much more. On the next turn round, I glanced at the table. Jennifer and Kim were smiling and twittering while Rain rolled her eyes and looked disgusted. For once in my life I really didn't care what they, or anyone else, thought. This was...perfect.

I know it was fast and maybe I should have been angry that he moved so quickly. After all, he didn't know if I was seeing someone else, but I guessed he just felt the same as I did. It was like time had stood still all those years ago and we were teenagers again. Whatever the reason, the closeness continued throughout the night. We got our own small table in the corner and he held my hand from time to time. We reminisced and caught up on old news.

Jimmy Whalen from Carmanville, Newfoundland was now James Whalen, one of the top brokers at the Toronto

Stock Exchange. I'm sure I would have felt ashamed of my lack of success had he not been so understanding, kind and non-judgmental. He realized that I'd just moved there recently and was sure I would get a better job. It was nothing like my parents would say about me cleaning toilets with a university degree. He got me, got my life. For once, I felt like I didn't have to explain; like I was wearing an old, faded pair of comfy jeans I'd forgotten about and found in the back of my closet.

The night moved on. I didn't know what the girls were doing. No one else existed in our world. I just knew that around 1:30 in the morning, Rain stomped over and announced they were going home.

"Not that you'd care or anything," she said, then trounced off again.

I didn't care if she was mad at me and I knew that the girls would understand. I explained to James about the transformation of my old high school friend after he commented that she sure had changed. He knew people like that too and didn't they just get on your nerves sometimes?

A few minutes later, we were encouraged to get out when all the lights were turned on and the bouncers announced it was closing time. I didn't want to leave him and he told me he felt the same way. I explained that Rain and I shared the cubby-hole, and unless he wanted to look at her crooked face all night, going to my place wouldn't be the best idea. His place, he explained, was the same. His roommate didn't like company much either. I suggested I call Jennifer and beg her and Kim to stay with Rain tonight, so I could stay at their place. James thought better of it. He held my hand and gently suggested a hotel he knew of. He was quick to explain that going to a hotel implied nothing. He didn't expect anything. He only wanted to spend some more time alone with me and didn't want the night to end. He wanted to talk and catch up, maybe see the sunrise after a night of talking. I was flattered by his attempts to be gallant but quite frankly I wanted a warm body that I felt comfortable with. I wanted to show him how much I'd learned since the back seat of his old Monte Carlo. Most of all, I just wanted to feel wanted.

The truth of the matter is that the night at the hotel ended up to be a lot of both. We talked, openly and deeply about our lives, our dreams, what we wanted and how close we were to that. We made love, intensely, again telling each other what we wanted and what our fantasies were. He was impressed with me and me with him. The sun came up and we didn't stop what we were in the middle of long enough to watch it. We showered together and he suggested we stay another day and night.

We didn't leave the room once. I called Rain to tell her I wouldn't be home, just so she wouldn't worry. I ignored her snide comments and politely said goodbye as she rambled on.

On Sunday morning, James told me he had to get back to his apartment. He had some work to do before Monday and really needed to catch up on his sleep. I had to work that night so I agreed. It was horribly hard to let him go. It took us both a long time to move out of each other's arms.

"I hope it's not another five years before I see you again," I said, trying not to sound pathetic.

"I promise it won't be," he said, and kissed me long and hard again. "I'll call you tomorrow."

Famous last words–I'll call you tomorrow. I suppose it's better than a general I'll call you. Either way, he didn't call. I was angry and hurt and felt like a complete idiot. I screwed his brains out all weekend and now he couldn't bother to call. I had believed him and now I looked a fool.

To call me crooked for the next few days would have been an understatement. Rain seemed pleasant compared to how I acted. I pretended we had agreed that it was a fling, but my friends must have seen the truth, at least Jennifer and Kim must have. Rain was still trying to get over the fact that I had sex with a guy I hadn't seen in years.

When Friday night came again, I wasn't in the mood to go back to the Rock, but there was a silly, insane part of me that thought I might see him there. He would run up to me and explain how he'd been in the hospital all week with a severe gastrointestinal infection or at an emergency stockbroker's conference. I still believed, somewhere deep inside, that it was fate and that there was a perfectly good explanation for him not calling. The truth was so much more unkind.

I was fairly drunk when he walked in, beautiful blond on his arm. He walked past me without speaking a word.

Something broke inside of me. I tried to resist the urge to run up there and rip her face off. Funny how we all blame and hate the other person who doesn't even know us and not the bastard who we'd slept with and was walking in with her. In the end, I thought the better of it. Maybe, who knew, she would be in my place next weekend.

After a few more drinks and being egged on by Jennifer and Pansy, I finally got up the nerve to walk over to him. I had debated what to say. I wanted to tell him off, but I also wanted to keep intact the tiny shred of dignity I had left. My anger won out.

Trying desperately to walk straight, I fixed my skirt and strolled up to the bar where the lovers were standing, drinking white wine in pretty glasses. The girl looked at me strangely when I stood up next to them and I hoped my eyes didn't look as unfocussed as they felt.

"Hi," I said to them both.

The girl turned to look at James. He smiled meekly and said, "Hi."

Before I had a chance to say another word James took over the conversation. "Lisa, I'd like you to meet my wife, Sharon. Sharon, this is Lisa. We were a little bit of an item in school. Puppy love, you know?"

His words cut me deeper than I ever imagined. He was married and I was a school kid fling.

"She's a cleaner up here now," he continued.

His tone, if not his words, turned the knife already deeply implanted in my back. I was a cleaner, one of the lower classes. A poor Newfie who had to take the shitty job to exist. She practically turned up her nose at me.

Up to that point, it was probably the single most painful moment in my life. The hurt was so profound that I can still feel it, so many years later. I looked at her and thought about him holding me, screwing me the weekend before, telling me how wonderful I was. Where was she at the time? She didn't know who he really was. As much as I didn't want to be me at that moment, I sent a silent prayer of thanks to God that I wasn't her.

With all the pride I had left, which I assure you was not much, I managed to say one thing before I walked away, never to see either of them again.

"Puppy love, huh? I think you're making too much of it," I said as I managed a smile. Be it anger or a lack of moral fibre on my part or just plain vengeance, the truth of the matter is that the look of pain and embarrassment on his face at that moment, is one of my most treasured memories.

The Book was Way Better than the Movie

Dear Mom and Dad,

Hello. How are you? Things are great here. Well, it really is a small world. I ran into Mr. Tobin the other day at Eaton's. Can you imagine? He was pleased to see me and we talked for a while, caught up on what I have been doing. He thought it was great that I was working up here. He is teaching here now and is writing a book. It is about being a teacher in Newfoundland so he should have no problem writing that. It was weird to see him as not being a teacher. I still felt like calling him Sir, but he told me to call him Bill. That was even weirder.

I've been thinking about getting another job. I still like Windmere but I'd like to get out of the industrial area of town and into the financial district. I have put in a few applications and I have two interviews this week. One of them is at *a marketing firm and they pay a lot of money to new employees and have a great pension plan. I think I would be great at marketing. Remember that poster I made for Aspen Cove Day? Sure, they still use that now, after about eight years. Anyway, I'll let you know how it turns out. Write me back soon and let me know how everything is going and how Taylor is. Give her a kiss for me.*

Love, Lisa

Everyone has one. All high school students have, at some point, a crush on a teacher. For all the guys at Rockwood High, the straight ones at least, it was Miss Vardy. Tall, thin, long blond hair, she was like a model with legs up to forever. For me and every other heterosexual female in our school, it was Mr. Tobin. He taught Language Arts. He was tall, muscular and gorgeous. Long brown hair, just past his shoulders, framed a beautiful dark face and the greenest eyes God ever created. But the best thing, the single best thing about Mr. Bill Tobin, was his posterior, his behind, his rear end, his butt, his derriere, or–as we all called it–his ass. Round and tight, it was perfect. He fit into the tightest jeans possible; I mean these were sprayed on. His shirts were the same: skin-tight, stuck to his oh-so-muscular form. White shirt and blue jeans every day. I don't know why he was allowed to even wear them, but he was and we were thankful for it.

Mr. Tobin must have known. Every dinner hour that he was on cafeteria duty he was surrounded by hoards of girls all waiting to ask more about Hemingway or the Tennessee Williams play we were studying. Like we cared. We gazed at him longingly and hung on his every word. Sometimes he would catch me staring at his crotch, that big bulge inside his tight jeans, and he would smile. I could never help it. My eyes just kept going there. He seemed to flex his biceps often when he stood before the class and always wiggled his ass when he wrote on the board. Sometimes he would turn his head a little and he must have seen at least five or six girls with their mouths open and eyes focussed somewhere just below his belt.

I was only employed as a Customer Service Representative at Eaton's for two days when I saw Mr. Tobin walk past the perfume counter where I was stationed. I had seen the position advertised in the *Globe and Mail* and applied right away, since I had decided cleaning toilets was not my chosen career path. The lady who interviewed me was a tiny thing who looked like she might break off at the slightest movement. I always tried to be firm in my handshake with potential employers, but I barely squeezed her hand as I was sure it would result in the sound of crunching bones and screams of pain.

"Do you know much about perfume?" she asked me in the interview.

Does Jovan Musk count? I wanted to ask. Oh, and I knew about Chanel Number 5 since my mom always hid hers in the back of her dresser drawer and would wear it only on the most special of occasions like Christmas or a funeral. I would sometimes sneak into her room and put a little on me so I could feel grown up and special. But mostly I wore Jovan Musk: subtle, oily and cheap.

I'd gotten the job and almost instantly regretted it. The overwhelming smell of all those perfumes seemed almost as bad as the toilets. I didn't think I had an allergy but I could almost feel my sinuses shrivel as each hour at the perfume counter passed. I debated staying there, but I had not given out any résumés for any office jobs in weeks so I had to stay. Maybe it would not be too bad.

Then I saw Mr. Tobin. I called out to him, much to the horror of the older woman who was training me. She turned quickly and glared at me over the top of the reading glasses perched on the edge of her nose. I ignored her and called out again. He stopped and turned toward me.

"Mr. Tobin?" I said, half statement, half question.

"Yes. My God, it's Lisa, Lisa Simms, right?" He looked shocked. More than that, he looked different.

He had gained maybe 10 pounds in the years since I had seen him and was even more muscular than I remembered. There was no flab anywhere. He was just more solid. His butt, at least from a side view, looked even more phenomenal than I remembered. It was fuller and rounder.

He walked up to the counter and grabbed my hand affectionately. He smiled and tiny wrinkles formed next to his eyes and his mouth. He was my fantasy; more mature, sexier than I remembered. I was 23 and he must have been all of 31. I remembered him telling us he was 24 when he taught us. Now I was almost that age and I suddenly felt like such a loser. How could he have had a career at 24 and here I was working at the perfume counter at Eaton's after quitting my glamorous job of cleaning toilets at night?

"You're here. In Toronto. Doing what?" he asked, his smile widening. He looked at me, at the counter. Before I could say anything, he said, "Stupid question."

"Just temporary," I reassured him. "I've only been up here about six weeks (okay, it was longer than that, but he didn't have to know). What are you doing here, Mr. Tobin? Buying perfume for the wife?" I just stuck my toe in and tested the water. I didn't dare dream that this man who I had had sex with dozens of times in my dreams could ever really fulfill them.

"It's Bill and I'm not married," he said simply. "You?"

I shook my head and saw it. He remembered my eyes on his crotch, on his ass, on his chest. I had been 16, off-limits to a teacher but I had sent him signals–licked my lips, traced them with my fingertips, leaned over with one button too many undone so he could see my perky teenage breasts. Seven years later, I saw as he sent those signals back. He remembered and he was up for it.

"I get off at 8:00," I heard my voice say, an octave lower than usual.

"Do you have a car?" he asked, his eyes traveling all over me, hungrily. I shook my head. "I'll pick you up then," he said. His hand brushed mine delicately and he swallowed hard.

I swallowed too. Just like him, I knew what was going to happen that night and thinking about it meant that I didn't notice another thing I did until I left the counter. Later, I would realize I sold more perfume to men that evening than any other day I worked at Eaton's. They must have known how turned on I was and responded.

I called Jennifer on my break. She squealed. She knew too. When I told her about his butt being even better, she said, "Imagine, you will be squeezing that tonight." I acted indignant and asked why she would think that. She said, "Because that's what I would do if I were you."

At 7:00, he showed up by my counter. He leaned against a rack of clothes and stared at me. There was nothing in the look except that he wanted me. I gave the same look back and willed the remaining minutes of my shift to go by. Mildred, the lady with the reading glasses, looked at him, then at me and fanned herself with the price list.

"Go on," she whispered. "But come in early tomorrow." She winked. She knew too.

Neither of us said anything after I walked out from behind the counter. He took my hand and hurriedly walked me to his car. Walking to the passenger's side I thought he was going to open my door, but he pushed me up against the car instead. We kissed hungrily. Still no words. We groped each other, exploring our bodies while our tongues danced together. He rubbed up against me, hard already, hard before I left the counter, I guessed. I was wet, ready for whatever the night would bring. Ready for all of my fantasies to come true.

Fantasies, as anyone who knows can tell you, are just that. When something you fantasize about for a long time–be it a sexual partner, a perfect job or your dream home–comes true it is seldom as good as you imagined. William Tobin did not even come close.

I'd imagined playing for hours, exploring everything with our tongues, lips and hands. I dreamt teacher teaching student, showing me more about sex than I could have ever conceived of. I anticipated fireworks. Mr. Tobin was a tiny firecracker that burnt out much too fast with only an insignificant bit of spark. The reality was that it was over 5 minutes after we got in the door of his apartment. I wanted an artist taking hours to create his work of art. I got McDonalds–in and out in 5 minutes–mission accomplished.

The first act disappointed me. The second devastated me. He rolled over, climbed out of bed–his back to me, his beautiful ass perky and glistening with sweat–bent over to get his pants, then pulled them on and walked out of the room. Still not one word. A friend of mine used to say of a certain four-letter word, that sometimes it was the only thing that fit. So it was that night with Mr. Tobin: I'd been fucked. So were my fantasies.

I never saw Bill Tobin again, not even in my mind. Some things are just never as good as you expect. Then again, maybe the things you dream most about can never live up to your expectations.

Best Laid Plans

Dear Mom and Dad,

How are you? I'm wonderful. I have a new job. I am a social worker. It is great. I arrange home care for people and advocate for them. It is very satisfying and we help everyone from retired judges to disabled vets. The people are so grateful for the help. I really feel like I make a difference.

I heard about the big glitter storm in St. John's. I would hate to be without power that long. As if all that ice everywhere was not enough, my friend Cassie got married in the middle of it all. You remember her, right? She lived next door to me when I had that apartment on Larkhall Street. She never worries about anything and went ahead with the wedding. No power and most of the guests did not show up but she did not care. They used candles for light and she said it was the most romantic wedding she had ever seen. Since she invited me, I got *her what I thought was the perfect gift only I am not sure about giving it to her now. I got her a really nice set of candleholders. I laugh at it every time I think of it. Maybe Cassie would laugh too so maybe I will send them. What do you think?*

That is all from here. How are things there? Give Taylor a kiss for me.

Love, Lisa

It sounded great. Leave the perfume counter at Eaton's and go to work at Sally's Home Care. I met Sally at a restaurant near the Rock. She was from Bonavista Bay and still spoke with a Newfoundland accent after 24 years. How could I not trust her?

She said I was perfect for the job. No longer would I be slaving away, cleaning toilets or making boxes or selling perfume to guilty husbands who either forgot their anniversaries or wanted to make sure their wives and girlfriends had the same perfume. I would be a personal assistant to elderly and disabled people. I would help them cook and keep them company. Occasionally I would have to help bathe and maybe dress someone. It was rewarding work, she told me. I would be their best friend, daughter, sister, mother; anything they needed. I had always wanted to do rewarding work, to give back to people whom life had been hard to and now, here was my chance.

I signed on, quitting the job at Eaton's. I went to a three-day course, at my expense, which Sally insisted I take. It included a sparse once over of first aid and CPR, yet I received a certificate saying I was qualified for both. We also learned how to safely lift someone in and out of a bed or bathtub. With these carefully studied methods we could easily lift someone with no risk of injury. I, along with everyone in the class, was more than capable of moving the dummies they provided us with. I named mine Clara. Clara was nice. Clara weighed all of 15 pounds. I liked Clara.

Three days and $250 later, I had a couple of new certificates and was a full-fledged member of the Sally's Home Care family. I proudly showed up at Sally's little office in the east end of Toronto. She gave me a list of names and told me that these were my clients for the day. I politely pointed out to Sally that there were fourteen people on the list. Obviously there had been a mistake. Perhaps four was the proper number since I had to spend time with them, get to know them and earn their trust. After all, I was there to be a part of their extended family, just as I had been taught in the course.

Sally explained to me that I was, indeed, to see fourteen people that day. That was my schedule and I would have to learn how to maximize my time. Sally must have noticed my shocked look and explained to me that I may have to wait for a less busy day to spend the quality time with the patients. I smiled, relieved that I would not always have to cram all these people into one day.

The hardest part of my task seemed to be getting to my clients. I didn't have a car so I had to use the subway, bus or taxi to get to each place and the appointments were spread out all over the city. I, along with my trusty map of Toronto, rearranged Sally's list as soon as I left the office, scheduling the people farthest from my apartment first so I could work my way back home. I smiled and realized it would not be as hard as I had first thought it would. I had already made Sally's list easier. I had to remember to explain this to her so she could make the lists simpler for her other employees.

The first name on my list was George Clents. He lived in apartment 308 in a building in downtown Toronto and my services were being paid for by Veterans Affairs. I was going to help a war hero. No doubt, he would enthral me with stories of bravery and horror as I cooked him a nice meal. No doubt, he would know how much I appreciated his efforts on behalf of my country and my freedom. He was 78, the list said and slightly hard of hearing. Sally, I was to find out, had a flair for understatement.

George Clents or, as I would begin to refer to him, the most excitable man I had ever met, lived in a beautiful apartment building. In the lobby a doorman ensured that I was expected. I should have seen the look of pity on his face, but I took it as admiration for my generous, caring nature. I traipsed up the stairs to the hall where green, plush carpet lined the floor. Opening the door, I saw that the first door in the hall was 328. Why is it that whenever I go through a door in an apartment building, I always start at the wrong end?

I walked down the corridor, admiring the brass fixtures, doorknockers and doorbells adorning the oak doors. Finally, I arrived at number 308 which looked exactly like all the other doors in the hall. I knocked. Nothing. I rang the doorbell. Nothing.

It takes very little to send my mind whirling into horrific visions of the worst possible scenario. Whatever you could think of as the worst thing that could happen, I would think something even more terrible. If an 8-ounce glass had 6-ounces of water in it, I would see it as one quarter empty. This is who I am. This is my curse. On that day it meant I pictured poor Mr. Clents almost dead on the floor of his apartment, his hand outstretched in a futile attempt to reach the telephone. If I was fortunate, I could reach him in time for him to give me parting messages for loved ones before he passed away. Taking a deep breath and praying a little prayer, I tried the door.

It opened. I cried out a greeting and waited for a response. I heard a small moan that enticed me further into the apartment as I closed the door behind me. I looked around and found Mr. Clents standing in the doorway of the kitchen. Mr. Clents was, to use a nice term, in his birthday suit. To be less nice, he was stark naked and swinging his penis around like it was a baton. Smiling, he looked me up and down then became–er, how shall I say this?–aroused. I was not flattered. In fact, I'm pretty sure a piece of wood may have turned his crank. Meanwhile, Mr. Clents was still shaking his love thing and smiling, while I stood there looking like an idiot.

Where was my war hero? Where was the friendly, loving, family atmosphere I had imagined? As I pondered these and other questions, Mr. Clents ran around the entire apartment, smiling and becoming more excited. Mr. Clents was very excited and it showed. Sadly, I don't remember ever seeing a man quite so equipped to show his excitement.

I tried to calm him down, tried talking reasonably, tried shouting a little in case he couldn't hear me, tried screaming at him to put his goddamn clothes on–all to no avail. He was having fun and I decided to say to Hell with it. Mr. Clents became number fourteen on my list and was still quite excited when I walked out the door. So much for my master list and master plan.

Next on my list was Delores Denton, a retired judge, my card said. She was 81 and lived with her daughter. Walking up the driveway to the luxurious mansion, I decided this job really required a car and that I would have to get one soon. I stopped at the gate and identified myself to the intercom.

The doorbell played "the Homecoming" as I waited on the front steps. I wasn't surprised when the help answered the door. An attractive man in a black suit asked who I was, then permitted me entry. Asking me to wait, he announced to someone in another room that home care was here. The house was spectacular. A gorgeous chandelier hung in the foyer. High ceilings with beautiful patterns carved into them dropped my jaw. An ornate banister and staircase led to an upper level. I couldn't wait to see the rest of the house.

"You're new and you're early," a voice said and I turned around to find a short, stocky woman dressed in a white nurse's uniform. "I'm Alice," she said. "I'm Judge Denton's nurse. Judge Denton does not have her bath until the afternoon. You are here too early."

I quickly realized that maybe Sally's list had been put in order of what people needed done and when. Now it looked like I had to return to two places later in the day and the time, trouble and expense of traveling all seemed a bit much.

"When can I come back?"

"Well, let's see if the judge will mind getting a bath early, not that she can let us know, poor soul. I guess it is okay this one time but you must come in the afternoon from now on. The judge likes to sleep late." Alice started to walk up the stairs and motioned for me to follow her.

"Thanks," I said. "I appreciate you letting me do this now. Can I ask why the judge needs me if she has her own nurse?"

"I don't do baths but I do help you with the lifting. So do Charles and Raymond. They are part of the house staff. I have to call them to come up."

The question of why someone would need four

people to lift her flitted through my mind in the second it took Alice to open the bedroom door and I saw Judge Delores Denton in all her splendour. The judge, it turns out, was no Clara. She was, to put it mildly, a large woman and I feared the four of us might not be up to the task. My training suddenly seemed laughable as I pondered how to even begin the job at hand.

Alice introduced us, explained that the judge had had a stroke and was incapable of speech or movement and left to call the extra lifting staff. I sat there, staring at this massive person with beautiful blue eyes full of pain. She was trapped in there, I felt. I think she knew what was going on. So I talked to her. I told her who I was and where I was from and how I ended up there. I told her what the weather was like and her eyes seemed to soften, seemed to twinkle a little. Maybe it was just wishful thinking.

I don't think the bath was an enjoyable experience for anyone. Once she got into a huge tub, I was left alone to clean the judge. Sally's course did not teach how to get into places hidden by masses of flesh and how to deal with bedsores so deep you could see the bone. I literally cried as I bathed those sores, and knew they must have hurt her so. Alice came in to treat the sores then we all lifted her back into her prison of a bed. I said goodbye to her and meant it. I would not be back there again, I decided then and there.

The rest of the day was equally awful with bedsores and unkempt people who smelled awful and didn't have the ability to look after themselves. I cooked a meal for a woman who cried when I left and begged me to stay a while longer since she was so lonely. Cleaning toilets that had no feelings, that endured no pain, seemed like a luxury.

With each appointment, my resolve to quit grew. I couldn't do it. I felt too much for those people and I was so sad. I think if it had been a hospital or an institution where I knew they had a certain level of care, it would have been easier but these people were in their homes, be they mansions or hovels, and seeing them floundering and miserable in their own homes was too much for me to bear.

At my second to last appointment, I called the office and asked for Sally who was unavailable. The assistant manager came on the line and I explained the situation with Mr. Clents and how he seemed to be completely out of it and how I thought I should get Social Services or someone in to help him. He didn't seem capable of living on his own and maybe needed to go to a senior's home.

"And who will pay for our services if he is in a senior's home?" she asked.

"Who cares? He shouldn't be on his own. I can't believe he's made it this long on his own."

"He has made it because of us. We manage and he is fine. Now, leave well enough alone."

"I'll call them myself then," I said, referring to Social Services.

"You do and you can forget coming to work tomorrow. This is a business and those people are our bread and butter. You don't ship them off elsewhere. They pay the bills, Missy."

"I want to speak to Sally."

"Sally is the one who ensures that Mr. Clents stays with us. I am merely repeating Sally's instructions. To quote her," she said, "'let the old man rot as long as we get our cut.'"

I hung up and called the number in the phonebook for the emergency Social Worker. I told her about Mr. Clents and that he really needed help. She said she would get someone around as soon as she could, maybe in a day or so.

That was my last act as a home care worker. I had quit a job and paid 250 bucks for absolutely nothing, for worse than nothing because the faces and bodies of the people I met that day would stay with me always and I wished I had not seen it. I wished I had not seen the pain or the nastiness of the people who wanted to make money off that pain. I knew most home care facilities were good places with kind people, but Sally's Home Care was awful and she robbed me of some of my naiveté.

I was now out of work again, so I crawled back to Eaton's and begged for my job back. They had no positions in perfume, but a cleaning job had just opened up in the company they contracted cleaning out to. Back to toilets. This puppy was getting tired of chasing her tail.

The Grass is Always Browner

Dear Mom and Dad,

How are things there? You will never believe where I went to this weekend. No way would you ever guess that I went out on a lake in a boat with a rich family. My friend, Randy, invited me up there with his family. No, Mom that does not mean we are serious. Still just more good friends than anything else. His father is a rich lawyer. I had a ball. They had a beautiful boat and we went out on the lake. It reminded me of being home except the spray was not salty. I missed the briny taste of the water.

I am not sure I would want to live the high life all the time but it was nice for a change. The people were all sweet. They made me feel right at home. I wish I had pictures. Their so called cottage was a mansion. It was huge. I would not want to clean it, though. Maybe someday I will have to worry about that, hey?

Oh Dad, the landlord fixed that leak afterwards so no need to worry about that anymore. I do not even know why Karen mentioned it to you. How are things there? Miss you both and miss Taylor. Give her a big hug and kiss for me.

Love, Lisa

I started dating Randy Hennerman in May of 1985. We met in a bar downtown where a bunch of us from my work had gone on a whim. It was a ritzy, expensive bar with more martinis served than beer. We had planned to stay for just one drink since it was all we could afford. That was before Randy locked eyes on me and decided he liked what he saw. He bought rounds for all of us so we stayed and got sloshed.

He was tall, handsome, muscular, smart, funny and rich–not that that would matter to me. Yeah, right. He took me to the best restaurants, the hottest nightclubs and paid for everything. It was kind of nice, for a change, so I went along for the ride. Somewhere along the line, I started to really like him. His grin made me smile and I felt better when I was walking beside him. I probably looked worse since this guy was really good looking: brown, curly hair, blue eyes, two big old dimples in his cheeks and great teeth.

He was perfect. Almost. He wasn't the best in bed. But I could work on him.

And work on him I did. Morning, noon and night we practiced as I subtly guided hands and lips and his tongue (just to mention a few parts) to where I liked them to be. He got better and didn't even realize it or how I had helped him. I hate doing that because then if you break up someone else gets the benefits of all your hard work while you had to trudge through all that mediocre sex to get to the pot of gold at the end of the rainbow. Just when it gets good, they're gone and you're back where you started.

After a couple of months, Randy decided he wanted me to meet his parents. He seemed excited about it, always giggling at the prospect of me getting together with the family. I was nervous at the thought. His parents were ultra rich. Daddy was a high-priced lawyer and Mommy was on the boards of the most connected charities. Their house was an eight bedroom Colonial in Richmond Hill and they owned another home and boat on Lake Simcoe.

We were going for the weekend to swim and boat and mingle with the upper-crust of Ontario society. Randy spoke of Senator so and so and Mayor such and such as close family friends from way back. I felt way out of my league but he reassured me that they were all really down-to-earth people and I would enjoy it there. I tried to relax, but I still felt ill at ease.

I was a little envious of Randy's easygoing lifestyle and ability to enjoy the good life without having to work too hard for it. I know, everyone says that money can't buy you happiness, but Randy seemed happy and rich. Plus, his parents got to enjoy a lot of luxuries I would have loved my parents to have. Still, my family always did okay except there was okay and then there was Hennerman okay.

On Friday, July 12, we set out for the lake. The day was cool for Toronto and stayed around 20 degrees. Randy drove his Mercedes from work downtown where he had gotten off early from his job as VP of marketing at a toy company. On the 401 we were bumper to bumper.

I was deep in thought on the ride up. I imagined my conversations with the Hennermans and their upper-class friends. I tried to remember words of Plato, Shakespeare, Churchill and Melville as we rode along, wanting to impress the clan. Randy reached over, squeezed my hand and told me not to worry; they would love me as I was. Then he said, "Like I do" and smiled. I was astounded. It had only been two months, after all, and he was already telling me he loved me, at least in a round about way.

Except for twice in my life, the 'I love you' thing always freaked me out. Do you respond back with "I love you too," maintain a horrible silence or change the subject? I squeezed his hand and lied. I said I hadn't even been thinking about his parents but about something I had forgotten to do at work; neatly changing the subject as if I hadn't noticed the implied words of affection. Besides, he hadn't really said "I love you." Totally different rules apply if they don't say those three specific little words in that precise order.

He squeezed my hand back and asked me to forget

about work. He wanted me to enjoy the weekend, he said. I smiled and promised I wouldn't think of work anymore. No further discussion of the "L" word. Another successful implementation of the old change the subject manoeuvre.

Cottage country in Ontario is a beautiful sight and something about it reminded me of home. It was the water, I think. The sounds of the boats, the look of the docks on the banks of the lake reminded me of the wharfs back home. The docks were smaller and neater, not meant to withstand North Atlantic storms, but they were by the water with little boats tied up and kids swimming around them. It felt comfortable. I looked forward to getting on a boat again.

The house on the lake, which they called a cottage, had five bedrooms, twenty-foot ceilings, three fireplaces, two decks, a two-car garage and hardwood floors. It was called "Hennerhaven." Yes, their cabin, their five-bedroom mansion had a name, painted professionally over the main door of the house overlooking the lake, the dock and their 36-foot cabin cruiser. Back home we named cabins something benign and unpretentious like "The Wellons" or "Home Away From Home" and it would be burnt into a little sign over the cabin door or painted in the stain left over from the picnic table. The Hennermans had a sign with beautiful, calligraphy letters surrounded by flourishes, painted over a serene scene of a sunset on a lake. It was, I assumed, the way to know the homes from the cabins. Stick a name on it, paint it on the house and call it a cabin. How quaint.

We were at Hennerhaven for fifteen minutes before I met his parents. Randy gave me the grand tour, which consisted of him pointing out things to me while I nodded and said "wow" or "interesting" or "pretty" or "cute" about things I really wasn't interested in. Oh, they were pretty and interesting and all of those things, but I wanted to meet the folks; get the butterflies out of my stomach. We finally found his parents on the main deck where they were already drinking scotch on the rocks and Moët champagne.

Five people sat in wicker chairs around a glass-topped table. They all turned as Randy said hello. I suddenly felt like the roasted pig at the luau. Everyone stared, looking me up and down without even trying to be subtle about it. His mother, who had obviously had a few glasses of champagne already, stood up with difficulty and stumbled toward us. I heard Randy mutter "shit" under his breath.

"Is this your Newfie friend?" she asked, saying Newfie like it was synonymous with maggot. Her hair looked an expensive brand of blond. Her face was that sad, saggy type that you could see she tried, with creams and God knows what else, to keep looking younger than it was. It was too moist, almost glowing. Dark circles rimmed her eyes and concealer filled the not-so-fine lines there. I guessed that in a year or two her denial would succumb to reality and she would shell out for the best facelift money could buy.

"This is Lisa," Randy said.

"Hello," she said, extending a sweaty hand. "MY NAME IS SA-RAH HENN-ER-MAN." She shouted at me.

"Pleased to meet you," I said, shaking her hand and

wondering what the Hell was wrong with her. This was way past drunk.

"Oh, my," she said, taking her hand away from mine and putting it over her mouth. The champagne in her other hand spilled onto the deck as she moved. "You speak English?"

"Mother," Randy sounded mortified. "Of course she speaks English."

"But Newfies speak Newfie don't they?" she asked seriously.

"Newfoundlanders speak English generally but some speak French as well," I said, not trying to hide my disgust.

"I am sorry. I didn't know. I've seen those interviews with people from Newfoundland on TV and the English subtitles come up as they speak." She was smiling, oblivious to how insulting she was.

"Newfoundland definitely has a unique dialect," Randy said. "But it is English, Mother."

"Again, I'm sorry." She turned and led us to the table. "This is Senator Tornig and his wife Laura," she pointed to a round, bald man and his painfully thin wife. Mrs. Tornig smiled weakly and I felt instant pity for her. "And this is Randy's father, John." He was an older, greyer, slightly wrinkled version of Randy and I couldn't help thinking he had held up much better than Randy's mother had. "And this is Trish Lane, an old and dear friend of Randy's."

Each person had nodded politely to me except Trish. She almost sneered at me. I felt defensive but didn't know why. Sarah introduced me as Randy's friend Lisa.

Trish huffed, laughed and turned away. I shot Randy a questioning look and he shook his head, as if to tell me not to notice her. But I did and I knew there was a story there. I was not, however, sure I wanted to hear it.

I was still reeling from the idea someone would think I couldn't speak English because I was from Newfoundland. Ignorance might be bliss but it was downright foolish most of the time. Next they'd probably ask me how big my igloo was.

John asked Randy if he wanted a drink and then assured me they had bought bottled beer especially for me. It was hot and I really wanted a cold beer, but they had assumed I would only drink beer and I hated such assumptions.

"I don't like beer," I said. Randy looked at me like I had ten heads. "Scotch will be fine," I heard myself say almost before I thought it.

I usually tried to stay away from scotch for two reasons; first, I didn't like the stuff much and second, it didn't make me a very nice person. I was what you'd call a saucy drunk when I'd had a few such drinks. I tried to start fights and said things to strangers and friends alike that generally got me into trouble. Looking back now, the decision to drink scotch that day may not have been the best one. But maybe it was.

I drank scotch number one while sitting around the table with the gang on the deck, making small talk about work. Sarah, it seemed, believed Newfoundlanders never worked and she commended me on actually toiling with the masses instead of collecting a welfare check. I accepted John's offer for another scotch and clenched my fist. Randy took my other hand and squeezed it as if to tell me to let it go. I politely said that Newfoundlanders are known as hard workers and then did as Randy wanted.

As John poured my drink, he spoke to Senator Tornig.

"Randy's pre-law degree may be put to some good one day, I suppose," John said. "For now, it seems we will have to accept this job he's playing around with. "Right?" John said, turning to Randy.

Randy nodded and looked down at the glass of scotch he'd hardly touched.

"He's vice-president of his department," I said and Randy smiled weakly at me.

"Yes," John said. "Everyone with a Harvard education should be so lucky as to sell dolls and teddy bears."

"Well, it's more than just dolls and..."

"It's okay," Randy said softly.

I glared at John as he passed me my drink and it seemed the subject had been dropped.

Scotch number two went down a little quicker than the first when we started to discuss my 'cute' accent.

"What is 'witten?'" Sarah slurred at me after I had said Randy had forgotten to take his swim suit witten.

"It's 'with him' said quickly," I answered.

"Make two words into one," Sarah said, laughing. "And they say you people are not lazy."

"Sarah," John interrupted. "I think you've had enough. Why don't you stop now?"

"Why don't you get me another drink," Sarah snapped. She turned to Randy and tapped his face lightly with an open hand. "You are such a good boy," she said. "You have always been so charitable."

I realized then, staring at the bottom of my empty glass that Randy hadn't spoken up once to defend me. He sat there and let her insult me, not saying a word. I didn't know whether he was a coward or just a mamma's boy, but either way I didn't like it.

There are certain things I cannot tolerate in people. Really wrinkled clothes bother me, comb-overs annoy me, prejudice disgusts me and cowardice irks me. Randy's mother was disgusting me and Randy was starting to go well beyond irking me.

I accepted the offer for a third drink but felt my resolve to play nice fading.

"Charitable?" I asked as I placed my hand a little too firmly down on the table.

"Oh, yes," she said. She was trying her best to focus on me–her attempt seemed sad. Everyone there knew she was pissed to the gills, but they pretended her desperate efforts to cover it up were working. "He always brought home little stray cats and dogs, even a frog once. You must have a lot of frogs there in Newfoundland."

"Some," I said as I gulped back drink number three.

"Isn't Karen Johansen's maid from Newfoundland?" she asked her husband with a heavy tongue. She turned to me. "You must know her."

"No, I don't think so."

"Really, but you all know each other, don't you?"

"No."

"Well, I was only asking. Is it part of your culture to be so rude?"

"Is it part of yours to be a drunken bitch?"

Oops, it was out there. No going back now. The thoughts whirling in my head had grown too many and one of them escaped through my mouth.

"Excuse me?"

"Lisa, I can't believe you said that," Randy chimed in. "What is wrong with you? You must be tired."

I could see Mrs. Tornig trying to hide the grin spreading across her face.

"Yes, I am tired," I answered. "Can we go back to the city now, please?"

"No, we came here to be with my family and I would like to stay."

"The gardener is leaving soon for the weekend. Perhaps you could ride in his truck with him. You'd feel comfortable there, wouldn't you?" Sarah said with a smirk.

Okay, up to that point I thought it had been complete ignorance and booze talking but I knew that last one was a shot at me. I stood up and opened my mouth to set my quaint Newfoundland spirit free.

"Lisa, can I show you a little souvenir a senator from Newfoundland gave me?" John asked, gently taking my arm and guiding me away from the situation.

He brought me to a room where an old map of Newfoundland hung on the wall. "You'll have to forgive my wife. The drink gets the better of her sometimes."

The drink was getting the better of me at that point and I told him I didn't know how he put up with her.

"There is only one way you put up with a woman like that, my dear. You have to find younger, more beautiful women who like the finer things in life and are a little wild." To my horror, he touched the side of my face. "My son has always had excellent taste."

Before I could slap his hand away and also possibly do major damage to his genitalia, I heard a voice in the doorway.

"Johnny?" the voice said and I was shocked to turn and find Trish standing there. John's hand quickly moved back to his side.

Trish's story suddenly became clear and I wondered how John had lured her away for the tempting offer. Perhaps he offered to show her a piece of art a senator had given him some years back before he stepped in to see how receptive his son's girlfriend would be to a little one-on-one action with the rich, powerful and almost famous. Whatever the offer had been, the look on her face said that she had jumped for it. I wondered if she had heard his line to me and if it had been any different from the one he'd used on her. Probably not, I guessed.

"Trish, dear, I was just showing Lisa…"

"I can see what you were showing Lisa," she said and walked away. John went after her and I was left looking at the map of Newfoundland and wishing I was there.

As I made my way back to the deck, there was no sign

of John or Trish. Sarah tried to stand up to talk to me. Instead she stumbled as her son, apparently well trained in the art of mother-catching, grabbed her arm and guided her back into the chair.

"Did my husband try to fuck you?" She tried to whisper but failed.

"Yes, I believe he did," I answered at the same time Randy said, "Mother, I wish you would not use that word."

Randy didn't even look at me, didn't blink an eye. His concern was not that his father had hit on me or that his mother had treated me like dirt but that his mother had used a four-letter word in mixed company.

"I want to go home now, Randy," I shouted. "Right now."

He lowered his voice as he moved closer to me. "Let's try to smooth this all out first, okay?"

"No, I don't think I will; thanks all the same. It seems to me you've probably been smoothing things out a lot of your life, huh? I mean your mother talks to me like I'm the missing link on the evolutionary scale while your dad liquors me up before he slaps the moves on me. All while you sit back and smile and close your eyes. How the Hell do you walk upright without a spine, anyway?"

Anger flickered in his eyes for half a second before he took control and politely asked me to leave.

"Is there a bus company, nearby?" I looked to the Tornigs and asked.

Sarah laughed and then snorted, an ugly sound, and told me that their kind do not need busses.

"I'll drive you dear," Mrs. Tornig said. "It is a beautiful evening for a drive." She smiled at me. "It is like a breath of fresh air around here."

"We just got here," the senator said.

"Yes, but I am leaving now," Mrs. Tornig said. "Thank you for a lovely afternoon, Sarah. We will have to do it again soon."

Sarah smiled half-heartedly. I could tell her head was getting harder to keep up.

I caught the vacant look in Randy's eyes and saw a lifetime of standing in his father's shadow and covering up his mother's drunkenness. My mother and father had never once made me feel like anything else in their lives was more important to them than my brother or me. I had thought that Randy's lawn looked so much greener than mine, but I could see all the brown patches there now and knew in my heart that I would not trade Randy's mansion of a cottage on the lake for my little house back home in Aspen Cove. Not then, not now, not ever.

Baptism by Fire

Dear Mom and Dad,

How are you? I am great. Guess what? I have a new job! I know I just started another job but this one is even better. I am helping addicted people at a counselling centre. I do assessments of them and set them up with counsellors. Do not worry. They are sober when they meet with me. That is a requirement of them coming to us. I know it is a weird job for me but it just felt right. My boss was blown away by me in the interview and hired me on the spot. So far I have had about twenty or so clients. They are all so nice and they are grateful for my help.

I love it! I am helping people every day and can see the results of what I do. I really never thought I could be making this big a difference.

How is Taylor? Give her a big kiss for me. (Oh Mom, I heard that Maggie Baker is *pregnant but she is not sure who the father is. I know Stella is not happy about that, now? After raising seven kids to have the last one pregnant at barely 16. My God.)*

Love, Lisa

Sometimes stuff just falls into your lap. I went to the Unemployment Insurance Centre and looked at the notices on the board. Not that I had not been thoroughly fulfilled as a coat check girl or waitress or pool cleaner or my failed attempt as a clerk typist (apparently you have to be able to type) or my latest job of file clerk, I mean how could I not be? I was working in an office. Yes, it meant the mind-numbing task of alphabetizing all the legal documents at the legal firm of Schneider and Schneider, but it was an office and it was air-conditioned. Of course, since it was late September, that particular perk of the job was a little late.

It had been over two years since I'd moved away from home and I still had a lousy job and an awful apartment with a weird roommate. I should have gone back to Newfoundland but I still felt like Rain needed me even though she didn't act like it and I still kept hoping I could find a job that fulfilled me. At least I had a chance here since there were so many more companies. Besides, I couldn't face going home with my tail between my legs only to admit that I couldn't hack it and that I'd been a failure. Worst of all, I would have to admit this to my parents who would wonder why I had left Toronto after I had told them about landing my latest good (and fictitious) job of Office Manager at a legal firm.

As I stood there, looking hopelessly at all the jobs I could have stayed in Newfoundland and worked at, a man came by and tacked a new card up on the board. Quickly my eyes stopped on key words–university degree; detoxification; psychology; addictions–all intriguing and promising as a career, rather than a job. I could help others. I could be a positive influence on people who needed my help. I could change their whole lives. Pictures of me looking back at smiling, grateful faces filled my head. I saw families hugging me with gratitude for saving their loved ones and for being so kind and generous. This, I felt certain to my very core, was my destiny, the reason I was put on earth.

No one was around so I took down the card and stuck it in my little purse. The address was on Dundas. As the bus neared my stop, I felt excited again and knew this was right for me. This job had to be mine (okay, so part of that certainty was the fact that the job card was safely in my purse and no one else had seen it but still, I felt positive).

The building was, in a word, ugly. Old concrete stood cracked and grey while huge, grey doors beckoned on top of rickety wooden steps. There was a larger than usual peephole in one of the doors. I don't know what I feared more–the uninviting doors or the steps I thought I would fall through. I felt small, looking up at the old, broad building and wondered for a second if this might be a bad idea. A voice inside my head said "turn around." I smiled and dismissed it, knowing that my calling was helping the many people who would stand on these steps with an even bigger voice telling them to turn around. How scary this must look to someone who has to start a daunting journey like recovery from addiction.

The buzzer startled me when I pressed it. A loud and sharp ring pierced my ears for the first of many times I would curse that bell. After a minute, I rang it again, even though I couldn't believe no one heard it the first time. After what seemed like too many more minutes, I rang once more just as someone opened the peephole and peered out. Then, the door flew open as someone stepped forward and looked at me with a scowl.

"What?" a tall, thin woman in overalls said. "The first thing you have to learn here is patience."

"Sorry," I whispered.

"What do you want?" she barked.

"Um, I want to see..." I looked down at the card, "Mr. Thompson?" It came out as a question even though it wasn't. "About the job."

"Humph. Got a degree, do you?" She turned and walked away, not waiting for me to answer.

"Yes, I do," I assured her.

She whirled around, put her feet apart, her hands on her hips and shook her head. "Well, I don't. You don't need a degree as far as I'm concerned. You need kindness and people skills and I am kind and I have people skills. Now, Thompson is down that hall, the third door on your right. There's a sign there that says, 'Manager.' I'm sure someone with a degree should be able to find it with no problem." She turned and walked away, leaving me in the hall to question both her kindness and her people skills–she must have been keeping them carefully hidden. I wondered if this was a test.

"Thank you," I shouted after her. No response. She didn't even turn around.

I walked down the hall and passed two doors–one said 'Meeting room' and the other said 'Family room.' The next door was marked 'Manager.' A piece of loose-leaf paper taped underneath it said, 'Benjamin Thompson.' I knocked tentatively.

"Come in," I heard from the other side of the door.

I opened the door to a tiny office, made more so by the sheer girth of Mr. Thompson. He was overweight–the kind of overweight that makes you wonder how he could move. His massive body squeezed into a tiny wooden chair so that much of him escaped over the chair. I felt sorry he did not have a better chair, as this one could not be comfortable. It was as if he wore the chair like too-tight clothing. I wondered also how the chair withstood the strain.

"Mr. Thompson?" I asked.

"Yes, come in." He didn't get up to greet me but I wasn't surprised. I was sure it would take a while to get out of and then back into the chair. I wasn't worthy of the effort, I assumed. I wondered what would be–perhaps a fire or a person screaming for help.

"I'm here about the job."

"That was fast," he said and laughed. It was a gentle laugh. The process of smiling made his cheeks spread upwards so that his eyes were no longer visible. The laugh made the large chin that sat more on his chest than atop his neck, wobble. He had kind, brown eyes and short cropped, black hair. His skin was pock marked, perhaps from acne and, once again, I felt bad for him. "I just called that in an hour ago," he said.

"I just happened to be there and when I saw it I knew it was the job for me." I had to sound confident. I had to persuade him that this job was made for me.

"Well, sit down." He motioned to another wooden chair. "Do you have a résumé?"

I passed him the pages I had revised since my move to Ontario. As he read over my paltry, and varied, work experience I studied the room. Smoke hung around like a fog. I guessed the walls were once white, but now they were nicotine-stained yellow. Two crayoned pictures were taped to the wall over his desk. The window was so dirty I couldn't tell if it even overlooked the outside or just another section of the building. A Bachelor of Social Work from Memorial University of Newfoundland hung on the wall.

"You're from Newfoundland?" we both said at the same time, then laughed. I nodded and Mr. Thompson said "yes."

"Small world," I said.

"The longer you are away from home the more you will realize how very small this world is." He moved slightly as if trying to get more comfortable. The effect seemed minimal. "So, what experience do you have with addictions?"

Mmmm, well, that was hard. Not really any but, well, maybe… "I worked in home care as you can see (even though I had only worked there a day, my résumé may have implied a longer employment). Many of our clients had addiction problems. Home care workers deal with drunk people all the time." It was true. I must have looked after four drunk people the day I worked with Sally. I had to scrape them off the floor, wash them and make them presentable so they could turn around and guzzle their booze again, messing up themselves and their surroundings, both of which I had just cleaned up.

Come on, tell him the truth, I thought. *Tell him your big body of experience with alcohol is yourself and your booze bag friends.* I've had a lot of my own experience. Night after blurry night of alcohol-induced regrets and hazy hung-over mornings not to mention the frequent assistance I've kindly offered my friends as I held their hair while they puked or made sure they were on their sides after they passed out. I've never shirked my responsibilities to clean up; I've even scraped the sides of cars after I yucked up out the window. I've been a shoulder to cry on and done my share of crying, all later in the night when the euphoria of intoxication turned to nostalgia for days gone by and friends lost.

"Plus some of my friends drink a lot and I have helped them out," I muttered, unsure if it was appropriate to say.

He nodded. "And what experience do you have with recovery in addictions?"

Recovery? I hadn't thought about that one. It is one thing to help someone crawl to their room while they're loaded, quite another to help someone make their way back from the depths of real addiction. I searched my mind for something I could bullshit into saying was experience in recovery. Waking my friends up after benders? Providing the hair of the dog that bit them the morning after the night before? I was good at that. I always had some hair of the dog around.

Then it hit me–the AA meeting I attended for a research project for my second-year sociology course. It was an open-speakers meeting and I sat there with the three other girls in my project group as I heard the inspiring story of a guy named Jake who had gone from a failed suicide attempt to an AA meeting and a life-altering encounter there with a fellow alcoholic.

And suddenly, in Mr. Thompson's office, there spewed from me the most horrendous and intricate lie about how I had gone to an AA meeting with my older sister (I don't have a sister) after I caught her attempting suicide and how she met a woman there who took her under her wing and helped her and became her sponsor. I changed some of the details of Jake's story, but kept most of them. I had to have this job. I had to help people and, anyway, the basics of the story were pretty much true. It was less of a lie than a fictionalized account of a true story, and no one ever minded those.

I explained how I knew the depths of addiction and the heights of recovery because of watching my sister spiral downward to rock bottom at the young age of 26. It was like it was coming out of someone else's mouth and I was sitting there watching myself blabber on about steps and higher powers. I knew Jake's powerful story that night had made an impression, but I was amazed at the detail I could recall. Finally, I stopped and sat back in the chair.

The rest of the interview seemed a formality. He mentioned that I had taken some psychology and social work courses. I explained how I had originally wanted to do social work, but had been disillusioned by its bureaucracy. I didn't tell him that I desperately feared public speaking and how almost all the social work courses at MUN involved class presentations. He explained that the detox, with the oh so original name of Hope House, involved some bureaucracy as well. I assured him I understood that and had learned to work within the system since I left university. He nodded.

"So, do you have any questions?" he asked. The poor man looked so uncomfortable in the chair I really wanted to ask him why he continued to sit in such a small, stuck to his body, chair. The question of how soon I would go to Hell for lying about the plight of nonexistent relatives flashed in my mind too, but I let that go.

"Um, does everyone working here have a university degree?"

"No, in fact this is something new. As part of our changing program here, we decided it would be better if we looked to hire university graduates." He smiled. "It is better for our reputation in the addiction community as well. Why do you ask?"

I considered telling him it was because of the evil bitch that opened the door and sneered about my schooling, but decided against it.

"Just wondering."

"When can you start?" he asked. I smiled and told him anytime.

My training at Hope House consisted of two supervised shifts where I was the third person on a two person shift. My two colleagues worked, like me, as Detoxification Attendants or DAs, a fancy title for puke cleaner-upper and general abuse taker. At least that's what it seemed like at first. Later on, I realized the help DAs could provide and respected the people who gave so much to others.

I was never so nervous as during that first shift. I probably never had it quite so bad as that shift either, or so it seemed. Baptism by fire, my colleagues explained and I was bathed in flames at the end of those first 12 hours.

Day one started quiet enough: reading dry operations manuals, learning the right way to complete the mound of paperwork required for each new admission and signing confidentiality agreements and other job related materials.

Bland words explained a myriad of policies, none of which, I would later learn, could match the unbelievably complex scenarios that could play out during a shift. The manual didn't tell me what to do when someone wraps their hands around your neck and starts to squeeze or how to deal with a nearly dead man in the shower. None of my training informed me how to react the hundreds of times someone would ask me to suck his cock or go fuck myself. Nothing I read that day told me how to act when blood oozed out from under a door so that you slid in it when you tried to get to the bleeder.

That first day, I got to the heart and soul of the detox at noon, just in time for the start of lunch. The pulse of Hope House could be found in what the brochures called, "the Sobering Area" and what the DAs, and most of the clients, called, "the Pit." Clients had to stay there a minimum of 12 hours so we could make sure they were completely sober, and relatively healthy, before they went into the residence. Alcohol withdrawal is a dangerous beast and seeing how badly a person was shaking in 12 hours helped us assess if he should go to the residence or stay in the Pit. Twelve hours was not always a great guideline as the worst withdrawal symptoms–the hallucinations and life-threatening delirium tremens, or DTs–came after about three days. Still, it was the best we could do and, by and large, it worked out pretty well.

At that time, Hope House only helped addicted men (they started to admit women in 1989) and all of our clients were coming off alcohol. The fact is that most of them were using the place to get a few good meals, a warm bed and a few days of rest for their booze-battered bodies so they could go right back at it again.

At noon, there were three people in the Pit. "This is our Sobering Area," Carl, my supervisor explained, proudly. "We have eight beds here. This," he pointed to a Plexiglas encased area in the centre of the room "is called the Observation Deck or OD. Here, we observe the people in the Sobering Area and this is where most of the work of the Detoxification Attendants takes place."

The ironically nicknamed OD was raised slightly above the rest of the Sobering Area so the employees inside could literally, and for some staff members figuratively, look down on the people sobering up. The Plexiglas surrounding the 12 by 9 room was severely scratched and dirty. The inside consisted of a long slab of desk–which took up about one-third of the room's width and its entire length–two files cabinets, a locked metal cabinet and three decrepit rolling chairs. Right away, my eyes went to the dark stain in the middle of the floor.

"What's that?" I blurted as I pointed to the stain.

"Blood," one of the as yet unnamed DAs said and smiled. "Don't teach you that in university do they?" he whispered as the supervisor spoke to the other DA.

I should also mention here that I was the number one guinea pig in an experiment at Hope House. Not only was I the first university grad there, I was also only the third ever DA of the female variety and the first female to work there who was under 40. I was blazing a trail as the flames from my baptism threatened to engulf me.

Carl introduced me to Bobby and Sue. Bobby was a balding short man who had more hair in his ears and protruding from his nose than on his entire head. Sue was a wide, pleasant looking woman with short peroxide-blond hair, steel blue eyes and a face unwrinkled by anything as emotional as a smile. They both nodded to me as they were given my name.

"So Lisa, you can just sit here while Bobby and Sue show you the ropes. They will explain what they are doing and show you where all the forms are. If there is an admission, you can watch, but we don't want you filling out any forms or doing any searches yet, okay?"

"Searches?" I naively asked. "I didn't read anything about searches in the manual."

"Well, it's there," Carl answered.

I hadn't seen that. Must have been the point where I got a little bored and skimmed over some, or maybe a lot, of the pages.

"We search everyone who gets admitted here," Carl explained after looking to the dynamic duo who just stared back at him. "We search them for weapons, drugs and especially alcohol. When I say alcohol, I mean anything with alcohol in it: mouthwash, aftershave, vanilla extract, Lysol. A lot of the clients will drink anything and everything when the craving for booze gets bad enough."

"Vanilla extract?" I asked. "And Lysol? You mean they would drink Lysol?"

Again Carl looked to my new colleagues and this time Bobby spoke up. "Drink of choice for a lot of the boys on the street."

"My God, that's sick. I mean they must be desperate to drink Lysol."

"They are," Bobby answered. "And so was I when I lived on the street and drank it."

I had nothing to say to that. Thankfully, Carl started his lecture again and filled the silence that Bobby's revelation had left behind.

"Any alcohol is disposed of by flushing it down the toilet or pouring it down the sink. The same with any drugs, which are obviously illegal or prescription drugs without a proper prescription bottle. We lock any contraband, like aftershave, in this locked cabinet." He pointed to the metal cabinet with a badly dented door.

"Big dent," I said, stupidly.

"Fist," Bobby said. "Missed my shift partner by that much." He placed his index finger very close to his thumb to show his partner's obvious narrow escape. "Got him on the second try though. Twenty-three stitches and a broken nose and five weeks off work."

I wanted to throw up. I decided I was going to go in, confess my lie to the manager, tell him I have no sister and wait to be fired. Alternatively, I thought I might run screaming from the building and pray I would never see it again. These people expected me to search men for weapons and contraband and hope they didn't hit me in the process.

I had never, ever had to use the word contraband in any job I had before. This was not the pretty, calm, helping-my-fellow-downtrodden-man job I had envisioned. This sounded pretty scary.

Before I could comment on the injuries of Bobby's shift partner, the huge buzzer doorbell went off, making me jump and squeal. "Lunch is here," Bobby said.

After lunch, Bobby and Sue gave me a rundown of the clients, in particular, Sal Pascatelli. Sal was on his third day of detox and was notorious for having seizures when withdrawing, usually on his third day. I had been informed how to handle a seizure–turn the guy on his side so he would not swallow his tongue and tell your shift partner so he or she could call an ambulance–and I knew this was a relatively common occurrence at Hope House. Still, my stomach knotted when I thought of it.

Bobby said we should check Sal every 15 minutes instead of the usual half an hour checks we were required to perform. If Sal seemed really shaky or at all forgetful or delusional, I should bring him to the OD for observation. That reassured me a little, but I found myself hoping that if Sal had a seizure, I would not be around. Ha.

It was 3:20 p.m. when I did my first solo check. Sal was in a dorm with four other beds, but he was the only one in the whole house who stayed in his bed all day. He had been there on the last check at 3:00, but I was a bit late doing my 15 minute check because of a new admission. There were three people in the Pit, all of them awake and drunk. Another person had been there, but he had threatened to kill me about two minutes after his arrival and the police, who Sue had called, escorted him out of my life for the time being.

I was surprised that Sal was no longer in his bed. I noticed a light coming from the bathroom in his room.

"Sal," I called out as I neared the bathroom.

There was no answer and that was when, to my horror, I looked down and saw the blood. The floor sloped a little and blood had run out from under the bathroom door. My once white sneaker now had a crimson sole as a puddle formed around it. I screamed as loud as I could and stood there, frozen.

Bobby arrived first with Sue only seconds behind. "Jesus Christ," Bobby exclaimed.

Since I had been blocking the doorway, Bobby pushed me roughly out of the way and ripped open the door. The floor of the tiny bathroom with stand-up shower was covered in blood and Bobby's first act upon entering was to slip in it and fall flat on his ass. His jeans were now soaked red and he yelled at us to call an ambulance.

Sal lay on the floor with his forehead and mouth split open. Two teeth littered the tile. At the time, I was at a loss to understand what had happened, but the pieces were later added together. Sal had had a seizure, hit his head on the corner of the Plexiglas shower door, then, as he fell, he hit the bottom edge of the shower stall, splitting his mouth open and knocking out his teeth.

Sue grabbed me by the shoulders and turned me to face her. "Call 911," she said slowly as she stared in my eyes. "Tell them you need an ambulance and what happened and that the person has lost a lot of blood." She was calm, as was Bobby who was sliding around the bathroom trying to tend to Sal. At the time, I was in shock and I couldn't even fathom having that kind of calm in times of crisis.

An hour later, Sal was in the hospital and I emptied the fifth bucket of red water into the custodian closet sink, then filled the bucket again. There was no custodian here, no security; the DAs did everything and the job of cleaning up the mess had fallen to me. Sue was looking after the Pit while Bobby showered and changed into clean clothes. He could not go home to change. No one was allowed to leave the building as that would leave only one staff member, and one person alone in the building could be in danger. I was not considered an official staff member until my training was over. The theory was that a new employee was ill-equipped to handle a crisis. I think I had just proven their point.

I threw up in the toilet twice when I began to mop. As I cleaned up the gore I thought about where I had come from and what I was doing. I had almost $15,000 in student loans; I had left my home that I loved more than anything to come to a strange place; and now, while living in a horrible apartment and cleaning up a bloody floor for the second time since I moved to Toronto, I wondered what the Hell I was doing there and why I didn't drop that stupid mop and walk out the door, straight to the airport and get on the next plane to home.

But, I didn't, because as much as I was scared and disgusted, I felt more alive than I ever had before. I thought about what my parents would think if they could see me mopping up blood and throwing up or getting threatened by someone who got so blotted that all he could focus on was his anger. I thought about it and put it out of my mind. I still had three or four buckets worth of work to do and knew this was the beginning of what would be the least boring job I could ever imagine.

The First Picture

Dear Mom and Dad,

How are things? Everything is good here. Work is busy but satisfying. No, Mom, I still haven't met any famous alcoholics. Even if I did, I couldn't tell you about it. Everything is confidential. How is Aunt Mary? Tell her that I said her hair will grow back. I even heard of people growing back curly hair when it used to be straight or hair that is a different colour. Tell her she might have long, curly blond hair in a year or so. I know you're worried, but I really think she will be okay.

Darren is doing great. He says hi. He is gone away for a week or so to visit an old friend who he has not seen in a while. I miss him (and you guys of course). Hope everything is good there. Give Taylor a kiss for me.

Love, Lisa

Darren Waters was a coward and I loved him. I say that with disgust, venom, disappointment, rage and a lot of love. I say it as I remember the two very different pictures of him I have in my head. The first picture is of Darren laughing and happy.

I met Darren in November of 1985. He was a mainlander and I laughingly told him I wouldn't hold that against him. We met at an afternoon hockey game when Toronto was playing Montreal in the old Maple Leaf Gardens. He was a Habs fan and foolish enough to shout about it while sitting next to me. I screamed twice as loud at him about him doing something I'm not even sure is physically possible with a hockey stick. He looked at me with surprise, then a flash of anger followed by a big beautiful smile.

He kissed me. Right there in the middle of the first period, the wonderful, smart, sexy Darren I would come to adore, reached out, grabbed my face and kissed me hard. It was a phenomenal kiss. Just enough tongue and more than enough passion. Maple Leafs be damned, I was hooked.

It probably helped that the Leafs beat the Canadiens three to one. It let me gloat for the four hours after the game we spent at a little bar on the east side of Toronto. He told me he was a struggling writer masquerading as a TV technician and I told him my story. He was from Orillia, loved hockey, acid rock, poetry and old movies. He was a man after my own heart and I felt at home with him.

Back at his apartment, he moved slowly. A brush of a hand on my cheek, a breath of air too close to my ear to be coincidence. He gave me white wine and read Kipling's "The Cat that Walked by Himself" to me, putting emphasis on words like "eat," "pussy" and "rub" as I anticipated what I knew was inevitable. This was fantastic foreplay and he had barely touched me since the first period of the game.

It was everything I thought it would be. His tall frame was muscular with well-developed pecs and biceps. His abs were less developed and he had a tiny paunch which looked strange on his otherwise buffed body. His tanned, angular face glistened with sweat. Long, sensitive fingers worked magic and his tousled dirty blond hair looked just right between my legs. Night turned to morning and I still hadn't had enough of him.

For five months, I never saw anything in his eyes for me but adoration. For five months he made me smile, laugh, and feel safe–never judging, never stifling me or acting jealous–he clicked with me and if he wasn't such a coward maybe we would still be together. But that wasn't meant to be and, really, who am I to judge the living Hell that was Darren's life?

In retrospect, as always, there were things I should have seen, should have said and maybe could have changed. I'm perfect at retrospect. I have everything figured out in hindsight. Maybe I'm a coward too, making everything into could-haves or should-haves instead of owning up to the fact that I stood by and watched it all unfold. But I digress.

Darren and I did everything together. We danced, had a ball lip synching at a little pub we found, went to hockey games, fought, made love, watched sunsets and sunrises, we even hiked and went ice fishing twice. Me. Ice fishing. I loved doing anything with him. He was full of fun and always made me happier than I expected.

He told me he loved me about four months after we met, during a particularly beautiful sunrise after a night full of talking and not so much talking. It came out so naturally, the "L" word didn't even surprise or scare me. I returned his words and we made love. The next day he gave me a necklace with a heart pendant. He had wrapped the chain around a key. He told me I had the key to his heart and he wanted me to have the key to his apartment. From then on, I spent most of my nights at his place. I was happy to get away from the cubby-hole and spend time with a normal person. He gave me space in his closet and one drawer, but I was careful. My parents would kill me if I moved in with a guy, so for now I would just sleep at his apartment and spend all my free time there.

It was five months post hockey game when I first saw it. I had arranged to go back to Darren's apartment after I finished an overtime shift at 11:00 one rainy April night. I'd been trying to call him all evening but with no luck. Still, we'd made plans and I picked up the Chinese food from our favourite restaurant and happily set off for a nice evening.

I let myself in as I juggled the bags of food and called out to Darren. There was no reply. The apartment was sparsely decorated, but at least everything seemed to match. The dark brown sofa looked fine (if boring) on the beige carpet and Darren's treasured orange beanbag chair was next to the tiny window overlooking an alley complete with a dumpster and the occasional prostitute servicing a client.

I set about warming up the now cold chicken fried rice, crispy fried won tons, sweet and sour chicken and chicken soo guy. Looking around for a note, I didn't see one. Oh well, I decided I would surprise Darren with a romantic night. Once I had put the food in the oven, I found a couple of candles that had already seen a few passionate evenings and grabbed two empty wine bottles for candle holders. As I walked into the bedroom I was startled by the sight of Darren lying on the bed, his body curled up in the fetal position. Tears streamed down his face while he rocked himself as if he was in pain.

"My God, what's wrong?" I asked, already horrified about whatever had happened.

"Get out," he whispered as something seemed to break lose in him and huge sobs racked his body. "Just leave me alone," he said, barely able to catch his breath between sobs.

"Whatever it is we can get through it together," I said as I knelt next to his bed. I moved to touch his hair but his words stopped me.

"Get the fuck out," a cold voice said as I stared into vacant eyes. "I want to be alone."

Now normally such a phrase would have caused me to exit stage right, *tout de suite*, and remind him of what I told him to do with the hockey stick on that first day we met, but something told me to stay. He was in a lot of pain and his words were coming from that hurt.

"Just tell me what's happened," I said, standing up again. "Just get it out. Say it."

But he didn't. More sobs, more requests to leave him, to just leave him alone. He told me to never come back and that I would be better off without him.

"If you don't tell me what's going on I will call your sister and find out. She'll at least know if someone belonged to you died," I said, tears now running down my face.

He rocked himself harder, curled into himself more and stopped crying. I shook him and screamed at him to talk to me, but he was gone–lost somewhere in a place I feared I would never want to see.

I had nowhere else to turn. I would have to call his sister. I had met her twice at a couple of parties, one Darren threw and one she had thrown. Her name was Julie. She seemed nice. She was a few years older than Darren and maybe a little overprotective. When I met her, she kept telling me how happy Darren seemed and how she hoped it would last. Julie wanted to know every detail about me and I sensed it was not just to be nosy. There were questions like had I done a lot of drugs and had I ever been serious with anyone before. These were questions to protect her little brother and, while I resented them, I appreciated that she loved him and didn't want to see him hurt.

"When you love someone," Julie had said to me, "you take them–warts and all." It made me wonder about Darren's warts because I'd always found it strange that he didn't seem to have any. He was smart, funny, financially comfortable, cute, patient, kind and sexy. I never saw him get mad or even lose his cool. He woke up in the morning with perfect hair and didn't even have morning breath. Darren had no downsides, at least not until that night at his apartment.

I felt uncomfortable calling Julie, but I didn't know what else to do. I looked up her number in his little address book and listened as long rings went through. It was almost 12:30 a.m. and no one likes to answer the phone at that time of the night. Nothing good ever comes over the phone after midnight.

"Is Julie there?" I asked sheepishly of the male voice that answered. It was Julie's husband, Chuck. He was a prick, in my opinion. He had hit on practically every woman, including me, at the parties we had attended.

"Who's this? It's after twelve, for Christ sakes," Chuck said. I could imagine his greasy black hair, slicked back in a way he must have thought looked cool, but really looked like he was a very unsuccessful Elvis impersonator. His baggy eyes and chinless face must have looked angry. I pictured Julie, reaching out and touching him to see what was going on, her short blond hair like Darren's and, just like Darren, a great body except for the little paunch. Chuck called her fat once at a party–I only wish I could be that fat.

"I know," I said, sounding even more pathetic than I had wanted to. Tears rolled down my face and the salt tasted strong on my lips. For a second it reminded me of home. "Look, I'm Darren's friend, Lisa and something is wrong with him. He's crying and…"

"Hang on," the prick said.

He must have handed Julie the phone because the voice that said "Darren's freaking out again," seemed farther away.

"Darren?" Julie's frantic voice said.

"No, it's Lisa. I'm at Darren's and he's, he's not well." As I spoke, Darren began to rock more violently, shaking the bed and making my last line a shoe-in for understatement of the week.

"Is he taking his medication?" she asked.

Hmmm, this was not good. I had expected her to tell me the family hamster had died or all of the Montreal Canadiens had gone down in a fiery plane crash; some nice explanation for why Darren was writhing around in sorrow on the bed, but not "is he taking his medication." This was probably not something I could help him with. This involved pharmaceuticals and I knew it was beyond my field of expertise.

"I don't know," I answered Julie's question. "What medication?"

"Lithium," she answered. I knew what it was from the clients at the detox who were on it and now I knew what I was dealing with. Lithium was used to treat manic depression.

The big question was why had I not seen any of this before? The answer was, of course, that it was Darren's manic part of his manic depressive disorder that I loved. The 4:00 a.m. knock on the door to tell me he was taking me out to Lake Ontario to watch the sunrise or the all night dancing or great insightful, rambling conversations we could have for hours. That, I had told myself, was just Darren's normal, outgoing and energetic self. But flip the coin to heads and you can suddenly see clearly what tails really looked like.

Manic depression or bipolar disorder as we call it these days: The disease where you are either on top of the world with all neurons firing so fast you can't slow down, or in such a deep state of depression that you're crying and rocking on the bed while your girlfriend calls your sister at 12:30 a.m. to realize the man she is in love with is mentally ill. Manic depression, where everyone loves you when you're up and no one knows you when you're down–not that you'd ever care about anything when you're that far down.

"Darren has manic depression?" I asked, knowing the answer already. I may just as well have asked if the ground gets wet when it rains.

"Goddamn it, yes," she said. I could hear her shuffling around and then the prick saying something about the nuthouse. "Look, Lisa, he is supposed to be taking lithium every day. He told me he has been taking it. He told me you knew all about his illness."

He had lied to me, lied to her about me–all so he would not have to take his medication. Why would he want to take it, though? It would stifle the part of him I knew.

"How bad is it?" Julie asked. "What is he doing?"

"He's on his bed. He was crying but he stopped. Now he's just rocking back and forth. He doesn't want me here. He told me to leave," I said. I wanted to add "so I'm out of here," but I couldn't. I loved this man and he was hurting, so I would stay and I would help.

"Then it is best you leave," she said. "Stay there until I get there, but then you should go. He needs to work this out on his own, maybe go back to the hospital. When he says he doesn't want you there, he really doesn't. He wants to be alone."

"Then why are you coming here?" I asked. It came out harsher than I wanted.

"Because I'm the one who takes away the sleeping pills and hides all the fucking sharp objects and shoelaces and sheets and bath towels so he can't try to kill himself again."

Words are amazing aren't they? Add one to another to another to form sentences then insert just one more like "again" and it changes everything. That little word in conjunction with the others can make your heart feel like it stopped beating and your knees grow so weak you just sit on the floor with a thud. My lover, my friend, my hyperactive boyfriend had tried to kill himself before. His sister was coming to prevent it from happening again.

"Oh," I said, unable to muster anything more profound. "Should I do that now?"

"No, just stay there until I get there. Turn out the lights because they upset him more. I'll be there in half an hour," she said then hung up.

In a daze, I turned off the lights in the rest of the apartment and noticed the Chinese food containers on the table, reminding me of a more normal time a mere 15 minutes before. I shut off the oven and returned to Darren's room.

"I love you," I whispered to him and kissed him on the forehead. Blank eyes stared somewhere else.

I sat on the floor, tears streaming, heart breaking and waited for his rescuer, his guardian, to show up and protect him from himself. I don't think I was ever in the presence of that much sadness until that night. I never thought I would be in the presence of more sadness, but I'd been wrong before.

Julie arrived in an angry blur of action, putting steak knives in a pillowcase she brought with her as she told me I could go.

"Are you angry at me?" I asked, being way too self-centred for this moment.

She slammed down the pillowcase and glared at me with eyes that had years of pain behind them.

"He's been fine for almost two years now and then you come along. You and your bubbly ways and party all night long lifestyle. Well, how the fuck was he supposed to keep up? You piss me off because he loves you and he wants to be normal because of that. I've seen it before with him. But what really pisses me off," she said, crying now, "is that I should have seen it. I should have and I didn't. Goddamn it." She punctuated each 'I' by slamming her hand on her chest. "I saw him hyper. He told me that it was just coffee and I believed him because I wanted to. Oh God," she buried her face in her hands.

"Please get out," she pleaded with me. This time, I listened.

The Second Picture

Dear Mom and Dad,

How are you guys doing? I am great. I have a little news I have to tell you, but it is not a big deal. Darren and I broke up. I am okay with it because we agreed on it. It just wasn't working out anymore. We will still be friends and there are no hard feelings.

Work is good and the apartment is fine. Karen says hi. She and I have been spending more time together now that I am not with Darren anymore. It is nice. I miss you. Give Taylor a kiss for me.

Love, Lisa

It had been a typical week. Go to work, party with friends, find out your boyfriend is mentally ill and tries to kill himself occasionally, have big blow out with boyfriend's sister about how you screwed up his life then get a call that he wants to see you in the psychiatric ward of a Toronto hospital.

The psych ward was a fun little spot with bars on the doors and windows and a wide variety of mental illnesses. Within minutes of arriving, I had seen an assortment of people I was scared of even as I wanted to tell them how sorry I was for their pain. "Pain" would be the word I would use to sum up the place. There was a lot of it in the faces of the patients and their families. I knew that kind of hurt would not just go away, but it could be treated with medications full of side effects that sometimes seemed worse than the disease itself.

I passed a man shuffling by the nurse's station. He looked up at me with hopeful eyes and said, "Mildred?" I gave him a smile reserved for times when I was at a loss for what to do or say. He repeated the name.

"Are you looking for Mildred?" I asked.

"Is she here?" he asked. He straightened up and his smile seemed to brighten his whole face.

"I don't know. I can ask the nurse."

"Excuse me," I said, tapping on the counter of the nurse's station. Three nurses stared at a chart and one of them looked up at me.

"This man is looking for Mildred."

She rolled her eyes and looked past me to the tall, gaunt, Mildred-hunter. "Mildred is gone home, Max. You know that." She looked back at me. "She's been gone for weeks now, but he keeps looking for her."

"Go on now, Max," she said. He seemed to shrink before my eyes as he hunched over and again started to shuffle along. I glanced back at the nurse who was once again focussed on the chart.

Darren was in room 386B. I walked down the hall and knocked cautiously on the door. Something inside me feared Darren would be that same hunched over man I had just seen, shuffling aimlessly and looking for something or someone he had lost. Part of me wanted to turn around and run the other way.

"Come in, come in, come in," a voice called out.

I opened the door slowly and peeked in. A man who looked to be East Indian or Pakistani jumped up and down and said, "Come in, come in, Lisa, Lisa, Lisa. Right, right right?" He looked to me and then to a bed where Darren sat. Darren smiled a little and nodded his head.

"Yes, this is Lisa," Darren said. "Lisa, this is Rasheem. Rasheem has been dying to meet you."

Rasheem was grinning and nodding. "Dying to meet Lisa. Dying to meet Lisa. Dying to meet Lisa."

"Hi Rasheem," I said. I waved but stayed clear.

"How about you give us a little space?" Darren asked Rasheem.

The man nodded again and then left, grinning all the while.

The room looked bland: white walls, white sheets and white floors with stains on them I tried not to think about. The faded yellow curtain separating the two beds in the room seemed the only hint of colour in the whole space. Even Darren's pyjamas were a drab grey.

"Hi," I said, staying back.

"Hi. You can come closer. I won't bite."

"Well, I know different." I smiled. It was the first time in days.

"I'm sorry. This must be hard on you." Darren looked down as he spoke.

"Hard on me? I'm more concerned about you."

"I'm sorry I didn't tell you."

"Me too. I could have helped."

"No, you couldn't have. You might as well understand that now. No one helps with this. It just is."

"But I could have made sure you took your meds."

"Ah yes, my meds. I asked them not to give me anything until later so I could be a tiny bit lucid when you got here."

"You're better than I expected."

"I'll be drooling an hour after I take my drugs. That's why I didn't take anything."

"But you will from now on, won't you?"

"You liked me manic. Hell, I liked me manic. I could write non-stop. A lot of it was crap, but I could still do it and some of it was good. I can't write a damned word on lithium. It kills the creative part of me; stifles who I really am. I can't do it. I'd rather die than take the stuff."

"Okay," I said, putting out my hand to shake his. "It's been great knowing you."

"What?"

"I am in your life if you take lithium, every day

forever. I am not in your life if you don't. I love you. I love you for who you are and I will love you regardless of whether you take the medication or not. But I don't want to see you like you were the other night again. So if you don't take it, I'm out of here."

"You won't like me with the lithium."

"I love you regardless, understand? Your choice."

But he was right. I didn't like him as much on lithium. I didn't like the normal, balanced Darren as much as the wild, manic one. He had a slight tremor the doctors kept trying to adjust his dosage to correct, drank water like he'd been in the desert for a week and went to the bathroom a half dozen times an hour. There were no more early sunrises for us to watch. I'm pretty sure that was as much my fault as the lithium. Maybe he would have gone out to watch sunrises, or do anything else, if I'd been more outgoing, but I was afraid of it all and assumed we had to have a quiet life. I started to spend more time at the cubby-hole and less at his place. I thought he needed his space. He must have seen that in me because after two months he changed.

I walked into his apartment at 10:00 a.m., expecting to find him in bed, but he was sitting at his table, pen to paper, writing like mad. Crumpled papers were all over the floor and ink was smeared on his face when he looked up at me. He hadn't written a word since his hospitalization, so I got worried.

"You okay, babe?" I asked. "You haven't written in a while."

"It feels great, Lisa. I'm so pumped. I got this idea and it started me rolling. I know I seem hyper, but I'm still taking the meds. I swear. I'm just so pumped about this story. It's great and the eight cups of coffee I've had haven't hurt. I had a dream and woke up at 2:00 and it's like this whole book was in my head. I've written sixty pages since then."

I flashed to the guy who cried and rocked on his bed sixty-odd days ago. I did not see the possibility of the manic stage. I just feared the depression again. I once asked him what it was like to be depressed. He told me he felt so awful about himself he was sure the world would be a better place without him. I feared him feeling like that again.

I doubted his explanation for the sudden surge of writing. I also believed him when he said he took the meds. I tucked my doubt away in a safe place named for a river in Egypt and watched the train barrel along down the tracks.

Four weeks later, after lots of writing rolls and alleged coffee highs and just being high on life, I had already confronted Darren on three different occasions. Each time turned out to be a big fight about how I didn't trust him. Darren would inevitably haul out the lithium bottle and demand I count them. They added up, of course. You don't play that game of bluff unless you're good at it and have flushed the daily dose. That particular day, I called Darren and he told me he couldn't see me. He said he had a cold.

He sure sounded stuffed up. He sounded down too, but so would I if I had a cold and wasn't I being just a bit too overprotective?

Darren and I were supposed to meet our friend, Ray Schwann for coffee that afternoon. Ray was a visual artist who was lucky enough to have gotten a small (very small) gallery to show some of his work so he had been working pretty much non-stop for weeks. It had taken a long while for us to all agree on a day to meet so I decided I would go along without Darren. Who knew when I would get the chance to talk to Ray again? I enjoyed his company. He was smart and artsy, but not pretentious and we had the best conversations. He was also one of the funniest people I had ever met. He was a high school friend of Darren's. I liked spending time with Ray so he could tell me how happy Darren was with me and how much Darren loved me and how he had never seen Darren like this with anyone. He saw Darren so rarely though, that Ray didn't even know about Darren's illness. Darren managed to keep it from most everyone in his life.

The coffee shop was small and Ray had chosen a table smack in the middle of the place so I couldn't miss him. He looked thinner than the last time I'd seen him and I imagined someone needed to remind him to eat while he was working.

"Sorry, Darren can't make it," I said. I kissed Ray on the cheek. "He's sick."

"Sick? Since when?"

"I talked to him a couple of hours ago."

"So did I. He just said he had stuff to do."

"What stuff?"

The waitress came with coffee pot in hand. We both accepted the coffee. Ray poured out a spoonful of sweet stuff from a canister of sugar.

"I don't know," Ray said. "He sounded weird." He stirred the coffee then clinked the spoon on the edge of the mug before laying it on the table. "Said he was going to make the world a better place today. He knew how and he was sure he could do it this time. I asked him what he was talking about, but he said that I would understand after he'd done it." Ray shook his head.

My mouth was dry, too dry to speak. I took a sip of scalding hot coffee and sputtered. I asked Ray if Darren had said anything else.

"Oh yeah, as if that wasn't weird enough, before he hung up the phone he said 'love you,' like he was talking to you or something. I laughed and started to say something back, but he had already hung up." Ray was still shaking his head and laughing as the world fell away around me. He was laughing and I knew already. I knew that this was the worst day of my life.

It was too late when we got to Darren's apartment. I let myself in with the key Darren had made such a big deal about giving me. There was a lot of blood in a bathtub and a razor. I can't describe the scene. There are no words. Use your imagination to fill in the blanks while I try to block the reality out of my mind. This is the second picture of Darren I carry in my head and wish to God I could get rid of somehow.

There was a note. Actually, there were three notes: one for me, one for Julie and one for his mother. They were exactly the same, four words, except for the name of the person it was addressed to. As you read it, just remember that Darren Waters was a coward and I loved him.

Lisa,
Sorry.
Love, Darren

Really, though, was there anything else for him to say?

Sugar Pops

Dear Mom and Dad,

How are you? I am good. Not much new here. Work seems to be getting busier and busier every day. I am not sure if it is good or bad. I hope it means that more people are looking for help instead of that there are just more people becoming alcoholics. Either way it means more people are getting help and that is good.

Thank you for the crimping iron for my birthday. It is exactly what I wanted. I use it all the time. I think I can throw my old curling iron away. All the girls use it when we're getting ready to go out. Except Karen. She's not really a crimped hair kind of girl.

Karen and I are talking about moving into a different apartment or maybe separate apartments. She likes a different crowd than me. I mean I love her to pieces, but we just live different lives with different groups of friends. She likes the artsy crowd and I like more normal people. Anyway, we are just talking about it for now.

How are you both? I was so sad to read your letter about Aunt Mary. Maybe the doctors in St. John's will be able to do more than the ones in Gander. Try not to worry too much, Mom (even though I know that you are). It will be fine.

That's all from here. Take care.

Love, Lisa

I've always been a fan of cereal but I never knew it would get me a roommate. Well, I guess the cereal and a twist of fate, or serendipity, got me a roommate. Not just a roommate, but a wonderful, memorable friend I never told Mom and Dad about. They would have never understood.

I went into a small corner store to look for a box of cereal. There was nothing in the apartment and I was sick of toast. The store didn't have much of a selection, only Sugar Pops and a bran cereal. Never a lover of bran, I went for the Sugar Pops but got a shock when I looked at the price. It was over a dollar more than it would be at the supermarket. "Talk about a mark-up," I said aloud, and I tsked.

"Sweetie, why don't you just go get a stick of butter over there and apply it directly to your thighs," a guy I hadn't noticed standing near me said. "Sugar," he practically squealed, "it is all sugar."

The man placed a hand on his skinny hip clad in skin-tight, black leather and smiled broadly. His platinum hair was crew-cut short except for the bangs that stopped just above his brown, mascara-laden eyes.

"Go with the bran, sweetie," he added.

I looked up and down his near emaciated form, taking in the leather pants and cut off black tank top under a thin mesh covering. He looked like a masculine (though not very masculine) Madonna of the "Like a Virgin" era.

I had just finished my third 12-hour night shift in a row at the detox. We had four admissions, all drunken twenty-somethings who could not keep their booze down which meant I got to listen to them alternate between vomiting (thankfully, their aim was good and they all managed to hit the bucket we provided), crying for causing me trouble and cursing me up in the heaps for not giving them cigarettes. I needed a quick and easy bite to eat before I lay my exhausted head on my pillow and this idiot standing in front of me was the only thing between me and kind unconsciousness.

"Who are you, the cereal fairy?" I asked. I could have cared less what he thought of my rudeness.

He cackled then squealed. "You go, girl. I like you," he said as he pointed his finger at me. "You're from home aren't you?"

"Newfoundland?" I asked, surprised. Not a hint of an accent from him.

"Oh yeah. You might as well wear a sign that says where you're from. I'm from Plate Cove."

"Aspen Cove."

He shot me a questioning look. "Aspirin Cove? What kind of a pill is that?"

I shook my head. "Look, I need sleep. I've been up all night and I have about three hours before my roommate gets up from her huge bed and starts making a big racket shuffling around the living room while I try to sleep on my uncomfortable couch."

"Are you serious? Really? It sounds like you need a new place to live."

Master of the obvious, I thought. Even strangers knew I needed to get out. But he didn't know about Dreg and what he'd done to Rain and how I didn't want to leave her on her own even though she refused to move to a bigger apartment or let me sleep in the bed. She hadn't even chipped in on the new couch I'd bought and I still paid half the rent. I had idiot written all over my forehead.

I shrugged and turned to walk away with my breakfast.

"So, how about it?" Mandonna asked.

"How about what?" I turned my head slightly toward him.

"Do you want a new place to live? My roommate just left me high and very dry and I need a new roomie, pronto. I like you and you'll grow to adore me. Nice two-bedroom with a bed and pretty good price on rent. How about it?"

I did a 180 and stared at him. He must have been able to see that idiot sign on my forehead. He actually thought I might move in with a complete stranger. Even as the thought that this guy was crazy for even asking me floated in my head, another thought (a crazier thought) entered as well. Maybe.

"Sorry, not interested." I dismissed my crazy thought.

"Hold out your hand," he said.

I'm not sure why I listened, but I extended my arm until my hand was right there in front of him, palm down. He turned my palm over, took a pen out of his pocket and wrote a phone number on my hand. The strange part was that I let him do it. This bizarre person was holding my hand and writing on it while I let him. Perhaps it was the fact that I watched him do this through bleary eyes, long past exhausted; it could have been that part of me wanted to leave the cubby-hole so desperately that I would do anything. The truth is that it was probably a combination of both.

"Call me," he said.

"Don't count on it," I replied, taking my hand back and walking away.

Back at the cubby-hole, I ate my sugary food before I curled up on the couch. I looked at my watch as I lay down; it was 8:53. I awoke to the sound of a frying pan being tossed into the sink at 10:34. Not even two hours.

"A little quiet, please," I yelled, eyes still closed. "I just got to sleep."

"Just cleaning up," Rain yelled back. "Not like some people."

Oh, how I wanted to turn over and go back to sleep, but I was awake now, as awake as at any time in my life. Actually, my anger was awake now and it wasn't about to turn itself off for my sleepy side to take over. I had no control over either Mr. Angry or Mr. Sleepy, but I knew Mr. Angry would win this battle.

"What the Hell is that supposed to mean?" Mr. Angry asked, hauling my carcass off the couch with him.

"This," she answered, holding up a cereal bowl. "You didn't wash it."

"I just finished another 12-hour shift. I wanted to sleep because I knew as soon as you crawled out of the bed, you and your singing and clunking around the house would wake me up. You have zero consideration for me and now you make a big noise because I didn't clean a bowl? One lousy fucking bowl? Jesus Christ."

Rain and I were like a couple who have been together too long. Everything she did seemed to annoy me to extremes and I'm sure she felt the same about me. The tiniest, most insignificant sound or gesture could explode into a huge fight. There were times, as rare as they were when we ate together and during each moment of these meals, my rage grew and grew. Ulcers festered as I clenched my jaw listening to her chew. Her jaw would click a little tiny bit and that enraged me. It was so bad that her breathing got to me which, I felt, she did much too loud. When someone's ability to live gets on your nerves that much, it's time to go.

I started to pull my hand through my hair and there it was, as clear as day–Mandonna's phone number on my palm, signalling like a beacon in the madness. It was an option, an out, a way I could do what I so desperately had wanted to do, and had ached to do since that first day she picked me up in downtown Toronto. As with all relationships that have reached the breaking point, my tirade erupted in volcanic proportions as I spewed out terrible things.

"Well, fuck you," I started. Her eyes widened with surprise then quickly narrowed as her face became a hateful scowl. "You have treated me like shit from day one here. You and that idiot boyfriend of yours. I saved your life from him, for Christ sakes, and what do I get? I pay half of the rent for this little corner while you sleep in the bedroom and never offer to switch places, especially after a night shift when you're out here banging around all day. You give me snide comments about my hair and my friends and what we do and where we go. You're just jealous because I have times when I have fun. I have times that I am allowed to not be a dark, brooding bitch like you, unhappy with the whole frigging world. It's like living with a snotty, pretentious dark cloud.

"It wouldn't even be so bad if you had a job that you could go to in the daytime but no, you can't give up your artistic integrity long enough to work. God forbid you become part of the lowly proletariat. Who the fuck even says proletariat any more? Only self-righteous, vegetarian, performance art creating, army boot wearing, shaved head, pierced everything, freaky bitches who want everything normal removed from the world. Well, fuck you and fuck this hole that I'm sick of living in. I've had enough. I've only stayed here because I didn't want you to be scared of being alone; scared that someone would beat the shit out of you again. You know I would have been better off if I'd left you on the floor that day…"

As I said it, I inhaled deeply and put my hand over my mouth. Her face, which had been reflecting an ever-increasing anger, suddenly looked hurt. She looked like a three-year old who'd heard someone whisper about there being no Santa.

"I didn't mean that," I said. "I'm sorry. I really didn't mean that."

"The problem is," she said, head held high, obviously fighting back the tears that rimmed her eyes, "I think you did. I think you meant every single thing you said." She looked at the floor. "Sometimes I wish you'd left me there too."

I felt so good and so bad all at once. My rant had relieved a pressure building for such a long time. But, I had said cruel things and wished I could take them back. I never wanted to hurt her like that and I really hadn't meant what I'd said. Sometimes, though, you can't unring the bell.

"You can keep the footlocker," she said. "I only bought it for you." As she walked back to her bedroom, I felt the urge to cry out, to try to fix this before I left, but I couldn't think of anything to say. Some wounds need time for the swelling to go down before you can bandage them.

One thing was for sure–we had both ended the roommate relationship. Her gift of the trunk meant we had gone past the point of no return. Quietly, I packed my meagre belongings. I left the footlocker. I knew I would never look at it without thinking of Rain, Dreg and the cubby-hole. I called a cab and dragged everything out into the hall. It took me ten minutes to get the lot of it down the five flights and onto the sidewalk where the cab driver helped me load my bags.

"Where to?" the cabbie asked.

I didn't know. I still felt dazed from the nasty battle. "Um, 185 Carron," I said. Jennifer's apartment. At least it was a port in the storm. I hoped I had enough money for the taxi. Just barely, it turned out, and none for a tip. Needless to say, the cab driver didn't help me lug my bags to the building.

"Uh oh," Jennifer said when she answered the door and saw me and everything I owned out in her hall. "This," she said as she shifted her weight to one leg, "is not good."

"It's Karnack, the magnificent, psychic seer extraordinaire." I said. "Can I come in?"

"For a little bit, yeah, but not to stay."

"I know, I know. I just need a figuring out place." Jennifer already lived with Kim in a one bedroom. Then Kim's twin sisters had come up a couple of weeks ago and moved in on the sectional sofa until they could find their own digs. I struggled to find a place to lay my belongings amongst the clutter of bags and clothes strewn around the living room.

"Ooh, maybe we could find a place for the three of us," Kim's sister Abby said. She bounced up and down on the sofa as she spoke.

"Yay," the other sister, Kat said. Her real name was Donna, but everyone called her Kat. I don't really know why.

Jennifer leaned backward and opened her eyes wide as if she had just heard my mom say to me, "Let's talk about my sex life." Then she turned to me and smiled an evil smile. "There you go," she said, "you should move in with them."

She knew it would never happen. Most people I knew barely tolerated the twins. I loved them, in a way, but could not abide them for any length of time. They were a special kind of stupid, the kind that was amusing for a short time, then annoying forever after. They were book smart, but had no common sense. They came over once when I was babysitting back home. I would walk the little baby, Carrie, around, point to things and say, "what's that?" Kat and Abby, ever helpful, would explain, "That's a television, Lisa" or "Well, Lisa, that is a teddy bear," spoken slowly so as not to confuse me. Abby once asked someone what time the midnight showing of a movie started. Kat called Kim at home once and when Kim answered, asked, "Where are you?" I could go on, but you get the picture.

"I have somewhere to live but I have to iron out a few details first," I blurted.

"Where?" They all said at the same time.

"Like I said, I have to iron out some details before I say anything. Now, can I use your phone?"

Jennifer gave me a look that said of course.

"In the room, if that's okay?" I added.

"Go for it," Kim said. "Not long distance, though, is it?"

I shook my head and went into the bedroom. I picked up the phone and dialled the number written on my hand. As the first ring went through, I realized I didn't even know his name. I was calling to move in with a person whose name I didn't know. Mom and Dad would die on the spot if they knew.

"Hello," a singsong voice answered. It sounded like Mandonna.

"Hi, I, um, I met you this morning in the convenience store by the cereal and you offered me a place to stay."

"To which you replied 'don't count on it.' Is that right?"

"Yes," I said softly. "Let's say things have changed."

"Well, you must embrace change to live fully so come on over to my place, sweetie."

"A couple of questions first. What's your name?"

"Clayton Ambrose Hiller, the third, but you better call me Clay. You?"

"Lisa Simms. No middle name you'll ever know. Okay,

now questions for my parents. Are you a murderer? A rapist? An escaped mental patient?"

"No, no and I was given an honourable discharge from each and every psychiatric facility I have ever been in."

Silence while I tried to figure out if he was joking.

"I was in the Waterford once," he added, referring to the mental hospital in St. John's. My parents put me in there when I was sixteen so some shrink could try to counsel the queer out of me. Didn't work."

"Where is this apartment of yours?" I asked. I felt scared and excited at the same time. I had a feeling I wouldn't be bored with this guy.

Comparing the cubby-hole to Clay's apartment is akin to comparing a beat up wreck to a new Mercedes. For one thing, there were two bedrooms. And a bed for me. When Clay showed me around, he said, "go ahead and try it out," so I lay on it, enjoying its softness and expanse. It was a double and more than twice the width of the little sofa I had slept on for so long. Laying there, blissfully enjoying the comfort, it suddenly struck me that I was splayed out on a bed with a complete stranger standing next to me. I hopped up and headed for the bedroom door.

"What?" Clay asked. "Bed bugs?"

"I don't know you and I was in a bedroom with you. That's crazy."

"Honey, you are safer in this bedroom with me than with any other man you've ever met. If you stripped naked and lay on the bed I'd still be focusing on that tacky hair cut and shoddy makeup."

"Oh please," I said. "You're wearing mesh, for God's sake." If anyone else had critiqued my hair and makeup I would have been crushed. Somehow with him I didn't care. He was a flamboyant, walking stereotype so, in my opinion, he was not one to judge.

He smiled and hugged me. "Want to know the rent?"

I nodded.

When he told me, I had to sit down. This big, bright two-bedroom apartment–made stylish by his flair for design–was only going to cost me fifty bucks more a month than the cubby-hole.

"How is this possible?" I asked when I could breathe again.

"I have a sugar daddy," Clay said grinning. "Well, not really, but I do have a nice older man who has moved to Tokyo for work. He should be gone at least two or three years, maybe more. He pays most of the rent as a house-sitting kind of fee while I keep the place looking lived in."

"Wow, that's a great deal. Why in the world did your last roommate leave?"

"We had a little disagreement about whether or not he should be screwing other guys in our bed." I knew he tried to hide the hurt, but it glared in his eyes. "Sooo, now that I'm rid of that bitch, are you going to be the new bitch of the house?"

Good question. I stared at this fork in the road. I didn't really have much choice and this would definitely be a big move. Moving in with a stranger, who was a guy, a gay guy, was not exactly something I thought I would ever do. This road meant a bed and a nice apartment and being in the middle of a completely foreign lifestyle. This road I was about to embark on looked a little scary, mostly because it was different. I didn't know how living with Clay would affect me forever, but I felt a twinge of excitement and a pang of fear at the same time.

Sometimes, if we could just see what it would be like down that road, we would turn around and run the other way. Thank God, we can't look to the future or I might have answered differently.

"Yes," I said and Clay squeezed me hard.

"This is going to be a blast, girlfriend," he said.

We had no idea.

Raindrops Keep Falling on my Head

Dear Mom and Dad,

Hi, how are you? I am good. I got your message on our new answering machine but have been so busy with work that I have not had time to return your call. I am writing this during my coffee break since it is about the only time I get. After talking to people all day, I really don't feel like talking when I come home. Also, I am doing a night course in communications. Got to try to get ahead all the time. I just got an excellent employee review and was told to keep up the good work.

How is everything there? Good, I hope.

Love, Lisa

P.S. The reason there is a man's voice on the answering machine is because Claudia, or Clay as she likes to be called, did a female self defence course and they recommend you *put a male voice on the machine so people will think a man lives there. Not that it's not safe here. This is a very secure building.*

Things were not going well. Well, the apartment was going well. I had been living with Clay for almost six months and I enjoyed every moment of it. Work was mostly the problem. Mr. Thompson had called me into his office for the third time in two months. He had received another complaint about my tone and demeanour while speaking to clients. I was just telling them the truth and not pussyfooting around like management wanted us to do. Most of the staff there wanted to say the things I said, and some of the others did say the same kind of stuff. I guess their tone was better than mine.

This time I had told a guy to stop bullshitting himself and accept that he had a problem. I had merely pointed out to him that it was not his nagging wife or his lousy job, but his inability to accept his alcoholism that kept sabotaging his sobriety. Mr. Thompson told me I was on probation and that one more warning would mean a suspension. He and I did some role-playing in his office and we went through some ways I could have expressed this sentiment in a less confrontational way. Mr. Thompson also suggested I complete a course in communicating more effectively, but I was still trying to put that off.

My eyes hurt when I left his office as I constantly had to stop them from rolling up in my head when Mr. Thompson told me to say things like "I feel that you are not taking responsibility because you are sabotaging your recovery" or "Let's search for ways you are preventing yourself from finding your true potential." These are nice, textbook phrases–good, decent ways to speak to people. The fact is, though, sometimes people need a kick in the butt to start moving forward, and I was being asked to shroud someone in need of butt-kicking in bubble wrap so he wouldn't be able to feel the kick. Defeated the purpose, in my view, but I had to play the game for a while so I could keep my job.

I knew Mr. Thompson wanted me to stay there and he was lenient with me for that reason. Hope House needed university grads, and there probably weren't too many who would stick with it. It took a particular type of person to work there–mostly someone who was a little crazy and had a long list of terrible jobs on their résumé.

It was a job of extremes. You were either bored to death waiting for something to happen or all out, full-on, insanely busy where you couldn't get a bite to eat or even have a pee. There were people who could touch your heart; who you would do anything for, and then there were people who tried your patience to the core; who you felt you could strangle with your bare hands. The weird thing was that the person you wanted to kill may very well have been the person you almost cried with the day before.

Generally, alcoholics, like the rest of us in the world, are nice people. They have families and try to stop the disease that infests their existence, but it is a tough thing to do. It is not as easy as just saying, "Okay, I'll quit drinking now." But, again like all groups of people, there are some nasty, mean bastards in the group collectively known as alcoholics and I had difficulty in restraining myself with them.

My training had made it clear that I was to be non-judgemental to all clients and after encountering one or two I strongly disliked (well, detested), I spoke to Bobby about it.

"That's okay," Bobby said. "No one said you had to like everyone. You just shouldn't judge them because of their disease. You're human, for Christ's sake."

Bobby, like all the other employees at Hope House except me, was a recovering alcoholic. My colleagues taught me much more about addiction and recovery than a million textbooks ever could. Stories and slogans from AA soon peppered my vocabulary and mentality. Most of my coworkers were the nicest people you could ever meet. Others were not, and I would come to despise them as much as I grew to love the sweet ones. Like I said, it was a job of extremes.

That evening, after getting off work and venting to Clay about how I hated trying to put tough love in nice wrapping paper, he and I decided that the best thing to do would be to get drunk.

The irony that I had somewhat lost control of my own drinking was not lost on me the numerous times I showed up at work with a hangover with the stink of stale booze on my breath. Since Darren died, I had spent a lot of time trying to prevent feeling my pain, or much of anything; trying to feel numb. This, since I didn't ever do drugs, meant drinking.

Clay was my friendly enabler and he helped me in my quest for oblivion by both accompanying me on the journey and providing plenty of alcohol for the ride. Clay, I had found out, had plenty of sugar daddies. Men seemed to love him and they showered him with expensive gifts and trips. He loved jewellery, but he only needed so much. As soon as a loverboy left the relationship (which they inevitably did–Clay was high, high maintenance in many ways), Clay sold off whatever expensive baubles he had garnered. So he did alright while never seeming to work. He had no job, but called himself a freelance writer. I didn't see him write once. I wasn't going to judge. My motto was to live and let live, oh, and bring on the Captain Morgan.

So, that evening Clay and I were sitting in the living room drinking rum and coke and smoking du Maurier cigarettes. He was regaling me with a wonderful story of his brother's struggle with Clay's sexual preference and how the brother always crossed his legs when Clay was in the room. I laughed so hard, I cried. I heard the security buzzer go off. I wiped my eyes while answering the intercom.

I said "Hello," which was followed by a sound that changed the expression on my face. A voice I would recognize anywhere said "Hello" back. It was Rain. What the Hell was Rain doing at my new, currently Rain-free apartment? I hadn't seen her in at least three months.

I didn't say a word. Finally, she said, "It's Rain."

"Yes, I know. Come up," I said as I buzzed the door open.

I turned around and saw Clay. His mouth was wide open.

"It's Rain," I said.

"I heard. Oooh, I get to meet the bitch. Why is she here?"

"I have no idea but it must be something big. I haven't spoken to her since I finally told Mom and Dad I moved out. I didn't have to pick up my mail from her anymore so there was no need to keep in touch. Jesus, I don't know what she wants."

It must have been five minutes before a knock finally came on the door. When I opened it, what had seemed like a strange situation suddenly became scary. Rain had two suitcases, my army footlocker and a cage sitting next to her in the hall. Her hair had grown out and was now past her shoulders. She still looked pale.

"I need a place to stay," she said with not even a "Hello" to ease her into the request.

"Um, well, come in," I answered.

Clay came up behind me and picked up the footlocker. He could barely lift it and placed it back on the floor to drag it in. His movement shook me out of my distraction and I grabbed a suitcase. Rain picked up the cage and left me to go back a second time to get her other suitcase.

"This is my cat, Patches," Rain answered my questioning look. "He is only two months old and I just can't get rid of him. Can he stay too?"

I introduced Clay to Rain and vice versa. Rain was quiet. She shook his hand and smiled.

"This is really Clay's apartment," I told Rain. "It's not mine to say whether you can move in. And it's only a two bedroom.

Clay got an extra glass from the kitchen, poured up a healthy helping of the Captain and passed it to Rain. She opened her mouth; then closed it again. I would have bet anything that she was going to tell him she didn't drink distilled liquor, but she took it and drank a swig.

"So, what's up?" Clay asked Rain. "You kicked her," he pointed to me, "out of your place after she supported you and now you show up begging for a place to stay."

I cringed. I knew she wouldn't be here if she wasn't desperate. I didn't think she needed the big rant.

She stood up and picked up the cage. I grabbed her hand as she reached for a suitcase.

"What is it?" I asked, "You did nothing wrong. So what is it?"

It was true. I was the one who had told her off. I was the horrible one who had said that I wished I had left her to die on the floor of our apartment. That she was even here after I had said something so rotten to her meant she obviously needed me. She had been there for me when I called to tell her I was on my way to Hell. My anger had mellowed in the past months. I'd been there at her lowest point and now I felt protective of her.

Rain's eyes filled and her lip trembled. I feared rust might set in if tears escaped onto all the metal pierced into her face, so I looked to Clay with my saddest eyes.

"If Lisa is okay with it, you and Patches can stay in her room. But you have to pay rent." She nodded her head. "And you have to tell us what happened. I need dish and Lisa is as boring as sin. Now you, you look like you have a ton of dish."

"It was a guy," she said simply.

"Oooh, now you're talking," Clay said. "What did this guy look like?"

"His name is Kieran." Clay shot me a look. "He is cute, strong; good body." I flashed to Dreg and the body she told me women would crawl over broken glass for. I put the visual out of my head.

"Mmmm, hmmm," Clay encouraged her. "Have another little drinkie poo."

Rain slugged another stiff shot of the Captain back and cringed.

Clay leaned over, put his elbows on his knees and rested his chin in his hands. "So what did the bastard do to you?"

"It wasn't him," she said. "It was me."

I sprang from the sofa. "It is not you. That's what that

scum-sucking pig Dreg made you feel, and now you think you deserve whatever some jackoff does to you, but that is not true."

"Go Lisa, Go Lisa," Clay said as he bounced up and down on the sofa.

"But it was me," Rain said. The tears that had threatened before came pouring out, spilling down her face and carrying an inordinate amount of black mascara with them. "I was the one who did something wrong."

Clay touched her arm and, to my surprise, Rain didn't pull away. She was not exactly a touchy-feely person, at least not with me or any of my friends. "What could you have done wrong, sweetie? Really, stop being so hard on yourself."

"But I did." She turned to look at Clay and only Clay. She was speaking to him now. I could have easily left the room. "I've been seeing Kieran for a couple of months. We got serious pretty fast and I moved in with him. It was hard paying the rent on the old apartment by myself," she glanced at me then turned back to Clay. "Well, the other night he was out playing a gig, he's a musician, and I was practicing a play." She broke down, sobbing.

Clay wrapped his arm around her and she wept on his shoulder. I felt like an outsider looking in on two old and dear friends. I was surprised for a second and then realized I shouldn't be. They were more alike than they were different. They were artsy–he an alleged writer and she an actor and playwright. They both stood out in a crowd and seemed to have given up caring what others thought of them. They both tended to speak their minds. It was weird to suddenly see that I had moved from one freak to another. What was it about me that made me surround myself with strangeness? Maybe I was a little strange myself.

After three or four minutes of her crying, Clay had finally egged her on to finish her tale; to fill in the blanks of why she was suddenly back in my life, and back in the place where I lived.

"I don't know why I did it. I really love Kieran but there was this guy in my play and he is tough, a real bad boy who acts like he doesn't care about anything. Rick. He asked me out for coffee and one thing led to another and well, we ended up back at our place, mine and Kieran's place."

"Yes?" Clay and I both leaned in further.

"And then in our bed. It all happened so fast and then we were in bed together and I was enjoying it. Rick was doing some amazing things and then..." She put her hand over her mouth and stifled a sob.

"Don't dare stop now," Clay said. Then he suddenly stood up and started jumping up and down. "Oh my God, Kieran did not catch you."

Her once again trembling lip answered for him.

"Oh my God," Clay squealed. He was enjoying this a little too much. As for me, I had mixed feelings. Rain had often judged me if I got to know a guy in the biblical sense a little too quickly for her moral measuring stick, and now here she was jumping in bed–her boyfriend's bed–with some guy she barely knew. But part of me felt bad for her. I think she was really screwed up: screwed up by Dreg and his abuse, screwed up by the bizarreness of her new life and screwed up by an anger that seemed to bubble under the surface in her all the time.

I looked at her. With her long, black hair and pale face, I guess she looked pretty in an anaemic sort of way. Someone else must have too. Two someones, at least. It was weird to picture Rain enjoying herself. Some people you just can't picture having sex and some people you just don't want to picture having sex. There was now a mental image in my head and I felt the urge to poke out my mind's eye.

"Okay, I know it is hard, sweetie but you must tell us every detail of what happened. It is the only way that you will feel better and can let this go," Clay said as he hugged her and winked at me. He opened his mouth in a big "O" to show me his glee at this little gossip session.

I felt a bit bad about her being Clay's (and my, to be honest) entertainment for the night. She was obviously hurting and this was no soap opera; this was a real person.

"Maybe she's not ready to talk about it," I piped up.

Clay slapped my hand. "Shhh." He furled his brow. "She needs to get this out. Now don't stop her." He looked at Rain and put his hand on her cheek (again, I could not believe she didn't pull away). "I'm here for you," he said and for a second, he seemed genuine.

She sighed. "I didn't hear him come in. I was, um,

wrapped up in what Rick was doing, (Ewww, yuck–there went my mind's eye) and then suddenly Rick was off me and on the floor."

"Oh my God." I swear Clay's eyes were on his cheeks.

"I jumped up and Kieran grabbed my hair. He called me a slut and told me to get out. Rick was crawling to the door and then Kieran dropped me and ran over to kick Rick in the stomach. He was kicking him over and over when I jumped on his back. Keep in mind that I was naked. (Please God, no, don't make me keep that in my mind.) So Kieran tried to throw me off and I screamed at Rick to run. He got out and then I jumped off Kieran's back. There I was, face to face with Kieran. He was so mad and I thought he was going to hit me, I thought he was going to..." she was racked in sobs and I knew what she thought. She must have been so scared.

The strange thing was that after I shoved Clay out of the way, I hugged her and the stranger thing was that she hugged me back. She cried on my shoulder and I told her I knew what she thought and that she was safe here. I motioned to Clay to leave and then when he resisted I told him, very calmly to leave us alone.

"It's okay," Rain said. "He can stay."

She cried a lot while she told Clay about what Dreg had done to her and how I had found her, near death. She continued to tell us how Kieran had spit in her face after Rick had crawled out of her life. She said the look of hurt and betrayal on Kieran's face hurt more than a hundred punches ever could. And she should know.

As Rain came back into my life, I accepted that she would stay there, at least for a while. She was my roommate again. And as I tried to imagine the wounded look she had seen in Kieran's face, I had no idea how soon I would see that same look myself or how such an expression could take my breath away.

The Boston Jersey

Dear Mom and Dad,

How are you guys? How is the weather there? It is perfect here even though I am sad summer is over.

Everything is excellent here. Kim's sister, Kat, went back home last week. We had a big going away party for her with a cake and everything. I will miss her. I am not sure her twin sister Abby will be able to stay up here without her, but she has a good job and should stick with it. Speaking of jobs, I got a raise. After two years you get a raise if you have done well so I got a big raise since my boss, Mr. Thompson, is always telling me that he has never had anyone quite like me work for him before. Anyway, that is all my news. Hope everything is good there. Give Taylor a kiss for me.

Love, Lisa

I'd heard about blackouts, you know the kind chronic alcoholics get. They drink too much and forget whole periods of time; sometimes days. I had only ever experienced what I call the black fuzzies. You would wake up after a night of way too many, and vaguely remember sections of the night before. Through a fog you could remember dancing with someone or saying something stupid when your inhibitions were low. Then some kind dingbat, usually a friend, would remind you of things you had done–embarrassing things you would have been more than happy to forget. "Do you remember that you danced on top of the table and stuck your crotch in that guy's face as you gyrated? How about when you called that woman a bitch, you know the one who wouldn't answer you when you asked where she'd gotten her coat? Don't you remember?"

Slowly, against your will, the fog would begin to lift and you could see the whole sad, embarrassing and sordid picture. You swear you'll never drink again, walk around with your head down for a while and, before too long, forget. That is, at least until the next time you got the black fuzzies.

That was true for me until a morning in September 1987, when I went beyond the black fuzzies and into the blackout zone. It was the first, last and only time I had a blackout and it was probably one of the scariest things that ever happened to me.

I had been out with several people from home–a couple of people from Badger's Quay, one from Bishop's Falls, Jennifer, Kim, Pansy, one of the twins–Kat (Abby had to work), and Mike, a guy Kat had been seeing for about six weeks. She was, she said, in love with him; as sure of it as she had been of anything in her whole life; as sure of it as she was about the last guy she'd gone out with just three months before.

Kat tended to dive into everything head first, come close to drowning then abandon whatever she'd been so into. Lord knows, I was like that too, but not to the extreme Kat was. She let everything else in her life go by the wayside as she obsessively followed her passion–a certain man, a certain course in university, piano, acting, singing, painting and any number of other various interests she'd had over the years.

That night we went to the Rock for a few minutes, but it was slow so we left to go to a house party of some people from Badger's Quay. I'd never met them before but, as with most people from home, we all got along like old friends. We started singing Newfoundland songs, like "the CN Bus" and "Aunt Martha's Sheep," while we drank more and more. The last thing I remembered, there were about eight or nine of us drinking a shot of tequila each, then a swig of 7-Up then yelling "shake," like we were mixing the drink inside ourselves. Kat started throwing up and, after a while, she and Mike left to go back to her place. Then the fog came in. Actually it is more like a curtain came down because no matter how hard I tried, I could never remember what happened that night. Maybe my subconscious blocked it out.

When I woke up the next morning, my first conscious sensation was the taste in my mouth. It was as if something had died and decomposed in my mouth. The second sensation hit me when I opened my eyes; I was hung over–painfully and severely hung over. Pounding pain shot through my head as the bright sunlight stung my eyes.

Next, I realized I had no idea how I had gotten there. I couldn't even remember leaving the party. Then I realized I wasn't home. The stucco on the ceiling I was staring at was nothing like the ceiling tiles in my room and the mattress I was lying on smelled more like my old sofa than my nice new bed.

I was naked, a sheet barely covering the left half of my body. I suddenly had a strange awareness; without even looking I knew there was someone else in the bed. Reluctantly, fearfully, I lifted my head ever so slightly. Glancing over, I saw a guy and was horrified I remembered nothing about what we'd done and how we'd gotten there. Both of us were naked so I could only guess at what we'd done.

I put my head back on the pillow and closed my eyes. My intention was to stop the pain shooting through my head and to make this guy, this situation, go away. It didn't work. The pain stayed and I was even more acutely aware of the guy next to me, breathing loudly, the sound of his breath banging on my head like a hammer.

I lay there, eyes closed, trying to figure out a way to get out of this situation and maintain a shred of dignity, until I heard him move. Before I had a chance to open my eyes I heard those two words every woman longs to hear when they wake up next to a new guy; "Oh, shit!" Opening my eyes, I repeated them only louder and with some extra, stronger words thrown in.

This was worse, much worse than I had thought. Not only was I in bed with this guy I couldn't remember sleeping with, but I knew him. Not only did I know him–he was my friend's boyfriend. I was lying next to Kat's boyfriend, Mike. The guy she said she knew with 100 percent certainty that she was definitely in love with. One thing I knew for sure was that we were both stark naked together in what I assumed was his apartment.

There was nothing, absolutely nothing. No matter how hard I tried, I couldn't remember one damned thing after the tequila. Mike had left with Kat. None of this made sense. My stomach was churning with too much booze and a huge amount of guilt and confusion. Running to the bathroom, I threw up some of the booze that was in my body and any remaining remnants of self-respect I may have had left.

Kat was like a little sister to me. True, I found her annoying at times. And true, I wondered how she could function with the apparent brainpower of a small rodent, but I think that made me love her more. I felt like she was a little, helpless, dumb animal that needed to be protected.

I always wanted to take care of her and to keep her safe from the many people who might take advantage of her stupidity.

I remembered when she was born. I was seven and my friend Kim was getting a baby brother or sister. She was excited and so was I. We would have a real, live doll to play with. Then Kim told me that there were two dolls and I learned about twins. Kim's mom, and the whole cove, had gotten quite a surprise after little Abigail showed up because soon little Kat (or Donna as she was still called then) followed. Everyone said it was a miracle.

Well, miracles are nice and all but Kim, and me to a lesser extent, soon found out that miracles can suck sometimes, literally and figuratively. Suddenly there were two little scrawny things getting all the attention, sucking on bottles, stinking up the place with filthy diapers and crying. My God, the crying. I remember Kim and me running out of the house with our fingers in our ears on more than one occasion. With two babies, it seemed if one was content, the other would be upset and that would, in turn, upset her sister who would join in on the wailing. Kim said it went on all night long and she spent many nights at my house for the next few months after the twins were born. My mother would always tut and say, "Poor Vera" about Kim's mom whenever she would see her. Kim's mom always had black circles under her eyes and her hair looked like she'd made an effort, but just hadn't carried it off.

I'm sure that in Hell there is a special place for the worst people, like rapists, murderers and lawyers where all they get to experience is crying babies. The crying of a baby is normally a horrendous thing, but it goes with a sweet smelling, eventually smiling little bundle of potential, which makes the crying worth it. But these evil people in Hell would get just the crying and none of the plusses. I often wish that part of Hell on certain people I meet (when Dreg dies he better get used to hearing "waaa").

Soon Kat and Abby became fun little playthings who did silly things and who we could blame when Kim broke the lamp that sat on her mom's bedside table. We pushed them on their little tricycles and sang silly songs while we dressed them. Once we thought we'd killed Abby when we pushed them both down a hill on a sled and the sled, with Abby in front, hit a tree. She lay in the snow for a while as Kim, Jennifer and I cried that we had killed her. When Abby woke up, her crying was one of the best sounds I ever heard and neither of us ever told Kim's parents about the incident. In later years, due to her lack of brilliance, I would've probably worried we had caused poor little Abby some brain damage, but since Kat shared the same denseness, I felt confident they both fell from the same stupid tree and hit every branch on the way down.

Anyway, the twins were really like my little sisters. But there I was in the bathroom of Kat's beloved, naked as the day I was born. Once I finished puking, the guilt was there as well as the dilemma of how I could leave the bathroom and go back in the room. I didn't want to walk back in there naked. I'd had sex with the guy–at least I thought I did–but that didn't mean I was willing to walk around naked in front of him in broad daylight. With any luck, Mike couldn't remember what had happened either and would forget the picture of my less than perfect body flailing around on his bed.

There was a laundry hamper overflowing with dirty clothes in the corner of the bathroom. Aside from the obvious visible evidence that Mike hadn't done his laundry in quite a while, there was the scent that confirmed the fact. It smelled like a locker room immediately after the big game. This made my only option even less appealing. But, I wanted to walk out there naked less than I wanted to wear one of Mike's dirty shirts. My stomach was still churning as I went through the upper layer of the clothes hamper. I found a long, mesh-type Boston Bruins hockey jersey and tried it on.

Looking in the mirror, I added to the shocks I'd already had that morning. I resembled a very hung over raccoon wearing a Bruins shirt. My hair, carefully sprayed and teased the night before, looked like what my nan would call a birch broom in the fits. I tried to flatten it down a little and washed my face. There wasn't a sound from Mike. I assumed he too was trying to comprehend what had happened the night before.

Finally, I got up the nerve to face him and try to find out what he remembered. I counted to three and threw open the door. I hadn't heard the opening of the apartment door, but Mike must have. He was still naked trying desperately, and unsuccessfully, to get into his underwear. Then Kat walked into the room.

The moment is frozen in my mind. Mike gave up and just stood there. I was decked out in his Bruins shirt. Kat's face crumpled and she let out a gasp, like someone had removed all the air from her lungs. I lost the ability to breathe. She kept looking at him then me; back and forth. No one spoke. Mike looked guilty as sin and I knew I did too. Kat looked like we had both smashed her in the face and I'm sure must have felt like it. I watched with amazement as she fought her feelings. Her eyes filled with tears, but before any of them could fall she swallowed, threw back her shoulders, walked straight over to me and slapped me hard across the face. "Slut," she hissed before she stormed out. She didn't even glance at Mike.

I understood why she attacked me and not him. The man didn't really matter. I'd broken a code among friends–you don't sleep with each other's boyfriends. The man was important enough to count as the instrument of the code breaking, but didn't hold a candle to the one who had broken it. I had done that.

Actually, I'd done it twice to be precise. At least that's what Mike told me after Kat left. He remembered bits and pieces, all wild and outrageous. I had apparently shown Mike the time of his young life and I had done things he hadn't even thought of (he gave details, but I won't). He had returned to the party after he'd dropped Kat off at her apartment. There came a point where he was holding the shooter glass I was drinking from in his mouth and somehow, in our intoxicated state, he would lean forward and empty it into my mouth. We had begun necking at the party and soon got a taxi to his place. According to Mike, the taxi driver had quite a show. My bra, which I could not find, was probably in the taxi, Mike told me.

He also told me how my friends–Jennifer, Kim and Pansy–had tried to stop me from leaving with Mike and how they were pretty pissed off with me when I left the party. How the Hell would I face them? How the Hell would I ever face Kat again?

Men, at least most I have known, have the remarkable ability to bounce back from the most difficult situations if sex is at all a possibility. Admittedly, Kat was gone, but I was still surprised when Mike said I looked great in his shirt and suggested that maybe we should go back to bed. I never said a word. I just took my clothes into the bathroom, changed and left.

I went to Kim's apartment. When I walked in, there was no doubt everyone knew what had happened. Kim was rubbing Kat's back as she sobbed on Abby's shoulder. I had opened the door with the key Jennifer had given me in case of emergency. They all turned to me at once and I wondered where the torches and pitchforks were. This was not good.

"Get the fuck out," Kat screamed. "Get out or I will fucking kill you." Tears streamed down her face as she squealed the words.

"You don't understand..." I started to explain but she held up her hand. I was trying to explain the inexplicable, ask forgiveness for the unforgivable.

"I don't care what you have to say. There's no excuse."

"I was drunk." My words sounded pathetic, even to me.

"You're always drunk. There's always some reason that you do the stupid things you do, but the real reason is that you're a drunken slut who screws anything she can. Everyone knows it and no one says it. We watch you, taking home every guy you see. Ever since Darren died, you screw everyone. And we talk about it all the time, amazed at how you can show your face after you fuck one after the other after the other. You are a SLUT. WHORE." She screamed as loud as she could. "And you're the only one who doesn't see it."

If the truth hurts then it hurts worse when people have thought about it and talked about it before, but never said it. I looked at Kim and could see she wasn't about to jump to my defence. This was true. My friends thought I was a slut and had obviously thought it all along. It was also true I had been sowing my wild oats in any field that would have me. A cavalcade of one-night stands went through my mind. As much as I had been using booze to numb my feelings about Darren's death, I had also been using emotionless sex to do the same. I was scared I would feel something, feared getting attached to anyone, so I made sure that hot, wild sex came before anything that could be remotely emotional. Deep inside me, I knew that.

But they knew it too. I was so much more transparent than I thought I was. I stood there feeling like I'd been punched in the stomach, wanting to defend myself. I couldn't. I could still see the look on her face when she'd walked into Mike's bedroom that morning. How could I argue that I wasn't a slut when I had woken up in bed with her boyfriend? There was no argument.

I started to leave. I opened the door to the apartment when Jennifer piped up.

"No, that's not the end of it," she said.

I turned around; waiting to see what was next, embarrassed beyond belief. Jennifer shot Kim a look I didn't understand and Kim looked away.

"You have never talked about it." Jennifer said.

"It just happened," I said. "I feel like shit. Worse than shit. I feel like a maggot. I don't even remember it. Kat, I beg you to forgive me."

Kat turned around without a word and went into the bathroom with Abby and Kim right behind her. "WHORE!" I heard come from the other side of the bathroom door.

"I'm not talking about today." Jennifer's voice was soft, her tone quiet. "I am talking about Darren. You have never talked about it. I, we, can see it's eating you up inside and you've never told us about it. Never talked about how it happened or what you saw or how you felt. You have to talk to someone about it, Lisa. I've never seen you like you've been lately. You need help."

I knew that, once again, they had all talked about this before. I hate it when people confer about me like that. I was angry even as tears stung my eyes. I felt something inside me break and I let it all come out. I had nothing to lose by talking now. I was naked again, stripped bare of everything I used to cover up the pain I had refused to share with anyone.

I started to cry and words came pouring out of me. I gave her the graphic details and told them how much it hurt. I told them about the screaming that was mine and the blood that was not. I told them everything and then agreed to go to a grief counsellor I had been referred to in the hospital after Darren's death.

The counsellor helped me and I went back to occasionally drinking a lot and sometimes drinking a little. I went back to dating rather than getting intimate once I knew a guy's name (first name; last name never seemed important). I went back to being me while Kat went back to Newfoundland. She never really forgave me and no excuses could ever make her. She decided to leave three days after I hurt her and I never even got to say goodbye.

Abby tried to stay in Toronto, but she couldn't live there without her sister.

I've seen Kat over the years from time to time, but we were never close again. She is married now and has two little boys and every time I see her, I feel like I'm wearing a Boston Bruins jersey and nothing else.

The Be All and End All

Dear Mom and Dad,

How are you? I am fine. Everything is good here. Karen's little cat got sick and we had to take her to the vet. She is okay now. The vet was a nice guy and he was from home. Deadman's Bay, I think.

Work is the same. Apartment is good. Clay helped me sew a hem in my jeans. She is good at that stuff, but I did pretty well too. She said I am a natural seamstress. Must turn after you, Mom. How is Uncle Sid? I know he must be lost without Aunt Mary and I know you miss her too. So do I although it's not the same when you're up here and don't have to pass her house every day. Tell Uncle Sid I am thinking about him. Miss you both. Give Taylor a kiss for me.

Love, Lisa

It was a normal morning, like any other. No, that's not true. It wasn't exactly normal. I mean Rain's little cat, Patches, woke me by puking all over my bed. The point is that it wasn't an absolutely amazing morning–the way you would expect an extraordinary, life-altering, life-affirming kind of day to start.

I was dreaming that a little yellow rubber ducky kept following me and quacking. Eventually the quacking started to sound more like coughing and I woke up to find Patches hacking up ungodly looking things onto my pillow.

I'm not exactly sure, but I am relatively certain I saw a hip joint, some vertebrae and some feathers in there. I imagined little songbirds and mice all digested and now sitting there on my pillow. I screamed Rain's name so loudly she ran into the room, saying, "What? What?" with genuine concern in her voice. Her worry for me disappeared when she saw Patches, retching and hacking. She went to him, hugged him and said his name over and over. I'd thrown up a mere three nights before and Rain had scoffed at me, telling me it was my own damned fault and that she had no pity for me. Now, all of a sudden, Patches hacks up body parts and she's gone all crazy with concern. I was swearing, Rain was crying and Patches was still trying–unsuccessfully–to get something else onto my pillow. Rain made an announcement: Patches had to go to the vet right away. A taxi would be necessary.

A taxi was an expensive proposition in Hell and reserved for emergencies. I argued that we could get the bus, but Rain insisted she would pay for it. I jumped at that since I didn't relish the idea of getting on a bus with a sick cat and a witch. I generally found the bus a peaceful place and I didn't want to deal with Rain's drama in the middle of a crowd. Rain put Patches in the cage along with a pillow from our bed.

Twenty-five minutes and approximately 3 ounces of cat vomit on my new, green pillowcase later we pulled up to the West End Veterinary Clinic. Rain was very upset at this point and almost shot out of the taxi before it stopped. I have to admit I was a little concerned about the fur ball too. He really seemed sick and I seemed destined to have it all over my belongings.

I paid the driver and asked for a receipt so I could make sure Rain reimbursed me for it. I walked into the crowded waiting room to find no sign of Rain or Patches. I asked the guy at the desk where they were. He seemed pretty unhappy with the "disruption," as he called it, that Rain had created when she brought her cat in. He said that Dr. Stagg, a Newfoundland name if I'd ever heard one, had immediately brought the weird young lady and the cat into the examining room. The guy sounded like he thought Dr. Stagg should be checking out the weird young lady and not the barfing cat. I asked if I could go in. He said I could.

The assistant led me to Exam Room 3 and opened the door. That was it; the end of my life as I knew it.

He didn't see me, didn't even look up from the inside of Patches' mouth where he was shining a light. Our eyes never met across a crowded room, or spotted cat, whichever the case may be, so you couldn't say it was cliché in that way. But something happened, something profound happened, when I saw him; my stomach flip-flopped and not just because of the big ball of wet hair sitting next to Patches. My palms got sweaty and my throat went dry and I knew. It sounds so corny and tacky but I knew, without ever looking in his face, that the sun would never rise on another day I wouldn't think of him; that I could grow old and be happy as long as he was with me; that my smile had been created for him; that from there on in, the world would be a more wonderful place just knowing he existed.

Then he looked up at me and smiled. I was sure I had melted and that the desk clerk would be there in a moment to mop me up. Dr. Stagg's eyes were deep blue and they smiled as well. Something happened with him too because he kept staring at me and smiling until Rain said something snotty like "Excuse me, but my cat is dying here." He assured her that Patches wasn't dying; she just had a hairball.

Again, he looked at me and smiled. "Hi, I'm Doctor Stagg, um Greg," he said. He looked like he was going to extend his hand to me but stopped himself. Since it had just been crammed down Patches' throat, I was thankful he did.

"I'm Lisa," I said, noticing that my voice had gone down an octave with no intention of my own. "I'm a friend of Rain's. I brought her here to get poor Patches checked out."

"Yeah, like you care about..." Rain started to say before I shot her a look that told her I would truly kill her if she said another word. It was the one and only time that particular look worked on her.

He smiled again and I noticed a twinkle in his eye that I liked. "Pleased to meet you, Lisa." I felt like it was the first time I had heard my name. I was sure I would never hear it said quite the same again.

"Me too," I said coyly.

"Anyway, Patches is fine," he said to me, ignoring Rain. "The hairball is up now." He turned to Rain. "You should add a little olive oil to his diet to prevent any more hairballs. You should monitor any vomiting he may do as well as his bowel movements. If you see any blood or diarrhoea let me know. Leave your number at the desk and I'll call in a couple of days to check on him."

"That's my number too," I said, feeling like an idiot as soon as it came out of my mouth. "We're roommates," I said sheepishly.

"Really?" he said, sounding surprised. Who wouldn't be? We made a strange team, as always.

"Well, thanks," Rain said, picking up Patches and cutting this ultra-important moment short. She walked to the door. I lingered, trying to walk a fine line between desperate and interested.

"Would you like to go out to dinner?" he asked, looking at me. My heart skipped a beat.

"Sure," I tried to sound nonchalant while I wanted to jump up and down with glee.

"Is tonight too short notice?" he asked. I shook my head and smiled. "7:00," he said, "at Mario's on Front?"

"I'll meet you there," I said. No discussion about that. I never got picked up for dates by guys I didn't know, no matter how great they were.

There were so many things to do that afternoon. Kim and Jennifer came over to my apartment to help me get ready. I babbled on to the girls and Clay about how gorgeous this guy was. He was at least 6 feet tall, light brown hair parted on the side and beautiful blue eyes. His smile was kind of tilted to one side. I told them he was the one, as I had about at least a dozen guys a hundred times before, but they believed me and I knew that meant something.

I fought the urge to be early and walked into Mario's at exactly 7:00. He was there already and waved to me when I walked in. I had on blue jeans I'd cut off too short while trying to hem them up but Clay had rescued them somehow by taking denim from inside the pockets or something and making a new hem. I also wore a white v-neck T-shirt, just low enough to let him know there were wonders underneath without being too slutty, and a blue and white cotton vest. My shoes were blue pumps with white tips. I thought I looked great. My hair was teased high on top and out to the side. I had shaved my legs, just in case, but I had a feeling nothing sexual would happen that night. My counsellor would be disappointed if I hopped into bed with someone on the first date.

He wore a turquoise T-shirt, beige linen blazer and

matching pants. He was going for that Miami Vice look and was very successful at it. His hair was fairly long and combed back. He'd obviously skipped a shave and had that scruffy look that was so popular then. My knees went weak at the sight of him.

"Hi," he said and I returned the greeting. "How's Patches?"

"Fine," I said. "Rain is babying him like crazy. He seems to hate it."

He laughed. It was one of those silent laughs that only created sound on the breath back in. "He's a cat and cats don't typically like to babied."

"Especially by Rain. I don't know anyone who would want to be babied by Rain."

He moved his fork around, trying to line up the top of it with the top of the napkin. Oh God, I hoped he wasn't anal retentive or obsessive compulsive or something. He was cute, a doctor of sorts, and seemed nice so far. Something had to be wrong with this picture.

"She's unusual, isn't she?" he said, almost absentmindedly then seemed embarrassed. "I don't mean that in a bad way," he said sheepishly.

"That's okay." I laughed slightly and touched his hand to reassure him. I didn't mean to do it. Not really. I just always did that. It helped at the detox. To touch someone gently often seemed to put them at ease. It was a habit. Greg didn't move his hand away. "She is unusual," I said.

I took my hand away. Not because I thought it shouldn't be there, but because it was too early in the date to hold hands. A touch was okay. A hold was not.

"We're roommates and old friends from school but somewhere along the way she changed. We're exact opposites."

"I could see. Probably good for each other." He smiled.

I smiled back, thinking he was mildly insane for even considering the idea. Rain and I good for each other. How foolish.

We talked for hours over food, wine, dessert, coffee and more coffee. He was from Deadman's Bay, not too far from home. He knew where Aspen Cove was and had been there a couple of times. He knew some Strattons from Ladle Cove. He had decided to become a vet when he was 12. His dog was put to sleep by a nice vet who helped his whole family, especially him, deal with the loss. He knew he wanted to help animals, and people, in that way. He had moved up here three years ago to get some quick experience and see the big city. He liked it well enough, but he said it wasn't home and never could be. He intended to move home as soon as he could.

Greg liked reading great books like Dante's *Inferno*, *Catch 22* and *Catcher in the Rye*, as well as science fiction and medical thrillers; liked Classical music, the Rolling Stones and Red Rider; and could talk about philosophy, religion, politics, history, old television shows and professional wrestling. I'd never met anybody else who had such varied interests. I could talk to him about almost anything I could think of. It was like I could finally let all of me out to one person. Before him, some of my friends liked TV and some liked books and philosophy and stuff. I could talk to them about some things, but not everything. Popping in a discussion of C.S. Lewis and *the Screwtape Letters* when you're watching the *Facts of Life* on TV doesn't go over well. Mention the latest episode of the *A Team* to some of the people I knew who would sit around and wax historical about early Christianity and they would roll their eyes in disgust. Greg Stagg could talk about anything and was interested when I spoke as well.

He asked me what I did for a living. I told him and he thought it was fascinating. He wanted to hear stories about my work and said I must be a special person to be able to do it. I told him a few of the more harrowing incidents at the detox, minus the names, like when a guy literally tried to jump me or when my shift partner had a chair broken over his head or the time I had walked in on a naked guy who complained to my boss that I had ogled his body. Greg laughed at times and seemed horrified in other places. I told him at least it was not a boring job.

The hours seemed to fly by and before we knew it, the waitress was giving us hard looks. It was clear she wanted us out so she could close up. We left to walk, not sure of our destination. He held out his arm, bent at the elbow, for me to hold onto. It felt right, walking down Yonge Street with him. A light snow fell and sparkled from the lights of the streetlamps. It felt peaceful. I felt safe.

Then, we were held up at knifepoint. Is it any wonder I still feel uneasy when everything in my life is going fine?

Every time I wasn't worrying–BOOM!–something would blindside me. Anyway, we were walking along, giggling over something silly I had said, arm in arm, my shoulder touching his so I could feel the warmth of his body. Everything felt good and then this young, pimply teenager stepped out in front of us from the shadows and pointed a knife in my face.

"Give me your jewellery and your money," he said in a squeaky voice.

Greg didn't flinch, didn't hesitate. He just let go of my arm and stepped in front of me, far too close to the knife for my liking. He was my protector, my valiant knight in shining armour. Somehow, his movement had scared the kid, obviously a novice at this, and the pipsqueak ran.

I stood there, in awe of what this man had done. I started to shake, my knees first then quickly, the rest of my body. I couldn't stop shaking. This pubescent male had destroyed my piece of mind, yet I never felt more protected.

Greg reassured me and hugged me. My God, he felt so good. I melted into him. We fit perfectly. I leaned back to look at him, to see the face of this wonderful man. I wasn't looking for a kiss. It wasn't on my mind. There were far too many other things playing around in there. But he reached out and touched my face gently with his hand. His mouth moved closer and mine moved toward him. His lips were velvet and mine became softer in his kiss. I knew I would never kiss anyone quite that way again, with quite that feeling. It was the perfect kiss; it made the whole world go away. People passed, I supposed, as we stood there kissing, but I didn't notice. I continued to shiver, more with pleasure than with fear. It wasn't a really long kiss but it felt like forever.

He asked if I was okay and I nodded. I couldn't speak. He walked me back to my apartment, again arm in arm. Somehow, I still felt safe. I'd deal with the panic of the hold-up later.

He walked me to my door, up the steps to my apartment and gently kissed me again. I didn't ask him in and he didn't give any indication he wanted an invitation.

"It's been a wonderful night," he said.

"Yes," I whispered, forgetting about the hold-up. I wanted the night to end there. I didn't want to go in and have Rain bug him about Patches or go back to his place and have the pressure to go further. Not his pressure, mine. It was perfect the way it was.

"Goodnight," I said.

"I'll call you in the morning," he said.

And he did.

The End of the Rainbow

Dear Mom and Dad,

Not much new here. Work is good and the weather is starting to get fine here again. I am sure it will start to get fine down there again in a couple of months.

How are you? I am pretty good. Just had a bit of flu, but am feeling much better now.

My roommate Clay left yesterday to go back home. Well, not really home, back to Newfoundland. She is from Plate Cove, but is going to St. John's since she feels like she could not live in a place as small as Plate Cove. She said she needs a city and even though St. John's is a small city, she figures it will have to do. I'm happy for her. Karen and I are getting used to it just being the two of us here now. Miss you guys. Give Taylor a kiss for me.

Love, Lisa

The day started okay. I had worked a night shift the night before and was about to start my long weekend; I had Friday, Saturday and Sunday off. Of course, Friday was a sleep day, but at least I had the rest of the day. I woke up at about 2:00 p.m. since I didn't want to sleep too late. God love Clay. When I walked out in my robe and slippers, looking bleary eyed, there was a pot of coffee brewing. I squealed and gave him a big old kiss on the lips.

"Ewww, girl lips, yuck," he said.

"Thank you for the coffee."

"Oh, that. I got it ready earlier and when I heard you in the bathroom I just turned it on. No biggie." He hugged me. "Are you tired, sweetie?"

"Not bad," I said as I rubbed my eyes.

"You look like shit."

"I know, I know, why can't I at least put on a little lipstick and mascara before I come out of the bathroom? Well, tough. You will have to continue to be exposed to my hideous, unmade up face." I patted his face. "I'm too lazy to look anything more than mediocre when I first get up, and most of the rest of the time."

"I know, but I have to try to make you look half decent. Anyway, you're beautiful on the inside. I'll just have to try to look past your hideous exterior."

"That's big of you."

I sat down to drink my big cup of coffee and noticed Clay looked weird. He looked kind of sad which is on a par with saying the moon is square. Clay never looked sad. He was the happiest, most annoyingly positive (at least about himself) person I ever knew. I called him my little rainbow since he always made everything look better and he had been the light in my life after the Rain, at least until the Rain came back.

"Is something wrong?" I asked, sure that it was not.

He said nothing.

"What? Come on, what is it?"

Still nothing, but he turned toward me and I saw a tear glisten in his eye.

"My God, what is it?"

He shook his head.

"Clay, what is it? Come on, tell me."

"I don't know how," he finally spoke up.

Oh my God, I thought, he's going to kick me out. He has been merely tolerating me and my mediocre face for too long and has decided he has a deep abiding loathing for me and it's time for me to move on.

"It's me, isn't it? You want me to move out?"

He smiled at me and gently touched my face. "You self-centred bitch; you just have to make it about you, don't you?" He laughed so hard the tears started to stream down his face and before I knew it, he was sobbing.

"Why me?" he said.

"Why you what, sweetie? What is it? Please tell me. You're scaring me." I stood and walked over to him.

"I have it."

"Have what?" but as I said it, I already knew. It was the same 'it' that hung over the head of every gay man (and lots of straight people too) in the 80s and my knees buckled. They literally buckled and I fell to the floor.

"I'm going to die, baby," he said and slumped down beside me.

He grabbed my hand and squeezed it, as he had a hundred times before. This time I had a sudden urge to pull away. It was 1988 and we still didn't know much about AIDS. The movie Philadelphia wasn't out yet; Ryan White, the little boy with haemophilia, hadn't died yet and the public mostly felt it was a gay disease. No one knew for sure how contagious it was; even though we had been told it was only transmitted through sexual contact. But there had been stories of people getting it through spit and sweat and here Clay had his hand, soggy from his own tears, on my hand.

I pulled my hand away. I still cannot believe that I pulled my hand away. One of my best friends ever had just been handed what was, at that time, a definite death sentence and I pulled my hand away when he touched me. There was silence and tension for a second and then I, hopeful I could cover up what I had so obviously done, stood up and said, "No, you must be wrong. This can't be."

He looked so hurt and I wanted to fix it and not feel bad so I reached down, pulled him up to standing and hugged him. I squeezed his little, thin, body so hard I thought he might crack off.

If he had noticed that I pulled away (and I will never know for sure if he did) he didn't say anything. He hugged me back and cried on my shoulder for at least a half an hour. My shirt was soaked with his tears and the truth–the goddamn awful truth–is that I could not wait to get that shirt off. I could not wait to get any remnant of my sweet, silly, beautiful, wonderful, crazy, friend off my body. God forgive me for that.

Clay had full blown AIDS when he was diagnosed. He was in Stage 4 of Non-Hodgkin's lymphoma and his bone marrow was affected. He had had symptoms, but he ignored them, tucking them safely into the river in Egypt until they made it impossible for him to deny them anymore. He had maybe six months to a year to live, he told me that morning. I couldn't breathe. How could this darling man not be here in a year?

After much crying and talking, he went into his room for a nap. He told me he had bad night sweats and would wake up soaking so he never really slept well anymore. He left and I grabbed the phone. I cried to Greg first, then Jennifer, who told Kim. Then I called Pansy and whispered the news to her. The last one of our little group to find out was Rain who came home from rehearsal to find me nursing a glass of the Captain and crying. I sobbed to her about the disease and his estimated time to live and how he had night sweats.

So many things in life can surprise you. So many things can sneak up and pull the rug from under you or turn everything upside down, any cliché will do, but sometimes something happens you can never, not even years later, explain. That was Rain. She handled it so much better than I did.

She went into his room, cloth in one hand and bowl of cool water in the other, and wiped his sweaty brow. I stood in the doorway watching as he shivered and said "Thank you" over and over while she wiped that cloth over his face, down his neck, onto his chest and around his stomach. She'd stop wiping at his stomach then dip the cloth in the water and start it all over. All the while, she held his hand and told him it would be okay. Told him we loved him and he would not be alone.

Suddenly I saw that Rain had been Karen all along. She was still the same person who, in high school after Sandra Coffey called me fat, managed to trip Sandra outside the school bus so she fell right into the mud puddle our bus driver always managed to park next to. She was still the person who came over to take me out when Simon Moss stood me up for a school dance (she even had a half dozen beer tucked away in the woods). This was the Karen who cried more than I did when my grandfather died. She was amazing.

Now, Rain became his companion, the person who helped him and reassured him while I continued to be his friend, more hands-off than Rain because she had taken over the role (and because I was scared). We had carefully delineated lines, which none of us discussed, but just seemed to happen. I was the joker, the flighty person who made him laugh and shared juicy gossip with him while we backbit everyone and smoked. Rain was the practical one; helping deal with symptoms and appointments, never fearing to touch Clay or his sweaty sheets.

I asked her once, in a hushed tone, if she was afraid of getting it.

"No," she snapped. "I'm not having sex with him, for God's sake. He needs us now. It's crappy to have people be afraid to touch you. Nan had TB when she was young and no one wanted to be around her. They would not eat off her plates or use the same toilet as her. She cried every time she told me about that and I swore I would never make anyone feel that way. And I won't. Not ever."

I thought about the one plate I put on the bottom of the dishes in the cupboard and always tried to use myself and quietly keep away from Clay and how I always cleaned the toilet seat with a little Comet before I sat on it. How could Rain be so much nicer than me about all of this? What did the fact that Rain was kinder and more non-judgemental than I was say about me?

One day Clay sat us both down, 'his two girls' as he called us, and told us he was going home to die.

"I know I never missed the place like you Lisa, but it is home and there are good people there; good people like you guys (massive guilt for me). It is just home and for some reason I want to see it again, to die where I was born."

"Well, your mom and dad must be happy you're going home," I said. Rain turned and shot me a nasty look.

"No," Clay answered. "I'm not going home to Plate

Cove. My parents don't want me there. They are afraid they will catch it and, of course, they still don't accept the fact that I am gay."

I looked at Clay, then to Rain, and realized she had become more than an appointment maker and sheet cleaner; she was a closer friend to Clay than I had ever been. He told her stuff–shared the deep, important things with her–while he and I merely liked to make fun of people or spend time judging their shoes. It broke my heart to realize it and to hear that Clay's parents could deny him. I started to cry.

"It's okay," he said. "There is a place I can stay where people will help me and I will be close to home. Anyway, I am sad to be leaving you, but it is only an exit a little bit earlier than the big one, so it is not so hard. At least you will remember me whole and a little healthy."

We bawled together for hours. Two days later, Clay left for Newfoundland. Rain and I were alone again in an apartment and we had once again been touched by something dark that made three roommates into two.

Clay lived back in Newfoundland for almost five months, the last of them spent in the Palliative Care Unit at St. Clare's Hospital. I only know for sure that he died because one of the volunteers at what is now called the AIDS Committee of Newfoundland and Labrador called me to let me know, as per Clay's wishes. I passed on the word to all his friends and we had a big party in his honour. We drank shots for him, told stories, laughed and cried.

He wrote his last letter to me three days before he died. I still read it at least a few times a year and know every word off by heart. This is it:

> *Hi sweetie,*
>
> *Well, this is it, honey. I am going fast. No pretty bows on it for you or bullshit to soften the blow. I am dying and this will be my last letter to you. I am too weak to write it and one of the amazing volunteers here, named Amanda, is helping me (she is telling me she does not want to write that she is amazing but I am instructing her to write down every fucking word I say, yes Amanda, including the word fuck).*
>
> *The volunteers here are so great. They show such love and compassion. It fills me with hope, even in the middle of all of this dark despair. They wash my clothes and read to me since my eyesight is pretty much gone. They laugh with me and cry with me. We laugh a lot. Sometimes, things seem so absurdly sad that all we can do is laugh.*
>
> *I feel like shit. God must hate us. I mean this is a living Hell, just waiting for the dying. I'll spare*

you the gory details, darling, but it is nasty here inside Clay's house of death.

I had a visit from family yesterday and I want to tell you about it. I know you hate it that my family has not seen me since I came back, but I saw one of them and it was spectacular. No, it wasn't my mom or dad or either one of my brothers. It was my 84-year old grandmother (Dad's mom) who got a bus all the way here from Plate Cove and slept on a cot next to my bed. In the middle of the night, I was asleep but was shaking and shivering and probably moaning when suddenly, in the middle of a dream I was having about being in a boat out on the middle of the ocean, something warm engulfed me. In my dream, a whale had swallowed me, but when I woke up my grandmother was holding me and rocking me. I have never felt so loved and I cried myself back to sleep in her arms. Can you believe that? Sometimes, even in the middle of a big pile of shit, you can find the most wonderful things. That is what dying has taught me.

So, I just wanted to leave you with a little advice. You worry too much and in the end none of it really matters. I want you to remember these two little words, Lisa, and every time you are stressed out about some unimportant thing like what someone else thinks of you or your job or your hair or even some of the bigger things like where the rent will come from, I want you to say these two little words: FUCK IT. I mean it babe, because it really doesn't matter and things will work out and things can get so much worse and even when they do get worse, maybe some old woman who smells like peppermint and pee can make it better for a few moments. So remember those words and remember me and that I adored you.

xxxxx

Clayton Ambrose Hillier III

I say those words still and often, but never enough because in the end–in the bitter end–none of the things we worry about on a daily basis ever really matter.

I sometimes worry that I was not a good enough friend to him and that, even though I don't think he ever knew, I didn't feel really comfortable with him in his hour of need. Occasionally, I wish I could have that time back and know more about AIDS like I do now. Maybe I would have been a better friend; maybe I could have given him the unconditional love and help that Rain gave him. But then, I remember Clay and just say, "Fuck it."

The Big Move

Dear Mom and Dad,

How is everything? Some news from here (finally). I have a new apartment. The old place cost too much without Clay so we decided to move. Actually, we moved to different apartments. Rain moved in on her own and I moved in with one of the girls from work. Her name is Rebecca, but I just call her Beck. We live just outside of Toronto in Mississauga. My new roommate has a car and I can get a ride to work with her. She even let me drive a couple of times. I can drive around Toronto with no problem. Hard to believe it when you remember the time I got freaked out by all the traffic and nearly wrecked your car trying to get out of the Avalon Mall parking lot. That was in St. John's, but I think the streets are more organized here so I can drive well enough.

My new address is attached. I had those nice printed labels done up and I thought you might like some of them. They are supposed to be for return addresses but you can use them when you write me. Anyway, everything is great. Miss you both. Give Taylor a kiss for me.

Love, Lisa

The worst thing about Toronto, among a very long list of bad things about the place was trying to get from point A to point B. The deceptive maps of Toronto were also used for the deceptive route layouts for subways, busses and trains and I never did figure them out very well. I always learned one or two possible routes to different areas and went that way, even if it meant it was the longest possible way to get there. Sometimes I would have to go to points R, S and W before I got to point B. Anything outside those familiar areas and I would have to write down precise instructions provided to me by maps in the Go stations and bus shelters. I managed and, as years went by, got better but I missed driving myself to places.

So, the first time Greg told me I could take his car to work I thought I had won the lottery. It was a Friday night and Greg said he would be sleeping anyway and had nowhere to go the next morning so I could use his car.

Since I was practically living at his beautiful, luxury apartment in Mississauga it seemed like this would not be a bad thing. After all, I had gone from his place to my work about a hundred times. How hard could it be?

The 401 is a fast highway and I always felt comfortable when the bus driver went over 120 kilometres per hour while weaving in and out of traffic. After all, I was safe in my seat, reading whatever book I was into at the time and staring at the same people I always seemed to see every time I rode the bus. If I was travelling in the morning, there were commuters, students, always two bald guys, at least one obscenely fat woman (who usually sat next to me) and one pregnant woman. While travelling at night, I shared the bus with at least one person who smelled like garbage and puke, a couple of people who looked like Rain and exactly one nice older woman who had a purse big enough to carry a dead body in. Actually, every bus ride had an older woman with a big purse. They must have been like bus security ready to pounce on people who stepped out of line and beat them with their purses.

Anyway, I was suddenly in the driver's seat on the 401 and totally in control of the vehicle I was in. Horns blew as cars whisked past me while I slogged along, doing about 80. Old men who wore hats passed me, for God's sake.

I was scared. There seemed to be sixteen lanes and that was only until I got to the exit ramps. I was sure there were more exit ramps than streets in Toronto. Greg had gone over the ride with me before I left, even though I had complained and told him I didn't need his help since I'd gone this route a million times and could drive it with my eyes closed. I thanked God that Greg's talking had drifted into my head since I vaguely remembered him telling me which exit to take and to make sure I changed over to the far right lane after I got to the beginning of the Don Valley Parkway.

Finally, I got into Toronto and was making my way to Dundas when someone turned out in front of me and I slammed on the brakes. A half a second later there was another slam; the guy behind me introduced himself to Greg's bumper. Uh oh!

The only thing hurt was my pride, but I freaked at the person who had hit me. I was swearing long before I exited the car and shut up when I saw a guy in a three piece suit with briefcase in hand, get out of his car. My mouth dropped as I saw John Hennerman, my ex-beau's father and the guy who had wanted to get to know me a little too well, get out of the car. I almost wanted to laugh. I mean it's a small world and all, but this seemed preposterous.

"Young lady, you cannot stop dead in traffic like that. This was clearly your fault. Now, I can have my lawyer here in ten minutes if you don't cooperate and give me your insurance information. As it is, I will have the police here in ten minutes who should charge you with reckless driving." He opened his briefcase, took out a phone the size of a small child and started dialling.

He didn't recognize me. I guess there was no reason he should. I was a barely a blip on his radar nearly three years before. Still, I had a lot of left over anger for him and the rest of his family, so I was kind of happy this was the guy who had hit me. The fact that he had decided to intimidate the 'young lady' he hit also encouraged me to speak my mind.

"Listen up, buddy." I pointed at his face as he put down his phone and opened his mouth. Looked like he'd suddenly realized who I was. "You hit me and you hit the back of my car which, as any idiot knows, means you're in the wrong. There are rules of the road about how many car lengths should be between your front bumper and my ass and you obviously disobeyed them or we wouldn't be standing here. So why don't we get those police here and we can compare stories. Maybe I'll contact a reporter or two and tell them how you tried to screw a poor working stiff out of the cost of your accident. Actually, now that I think of it, I could also tell them how you tried to screw a poor working stiff, period. Please don't make me get nasty."

Oh, he recognized me alright. He could not give me his information fast enough and he offered me a tremendous amount of money to settle this there and then. I told him that insurance would be fine and asked him to call Greg to tell him what happened since it was Greg's car. He offered me the use of his phone. I quickly called Greg and asked him to call my work and explain that I wouldn't be in. My neck was sore, I said loud enough for

Mr. Hennerman to grow two shades paler.

Greg wasn't angry. As a matter of fact, he was relieved I was okay (and a little surprised at how accommodating the man who had hit me was being). He hugged me and told me how important I was to him. He had gotten a taxi there and he drove back home (thank God) while I tried to calm down a little. I'm not sure if it was the accident or seeing Hennerman again, but I was shaking like a leaf.

When we got through Greg's apartment door, he turned and kissed me hard. He pulled away and said those three words I had been waiting to hear so I could say them back to him (well, I wasn't going to say it first).

"I love you," he said as he looked into my eyes.

"I love you, too," I happily responded.

The next forty-five minutes or so were amazingly good at making my sore neck (and all the rest of me) feel better. As I lit a cigarette in bed, Greg told me he needed to ask me something important.

"This is a big question and will be a big move if you answer yes," he told me.

I stopped breathing as I turned toward him and searched his face to see if he was serious. I loved him and wanted to be with him all the time, but I thought marriage would mean a big change that I wasn't ready for. I had only known him for four months and I wasn't sure I wanted to be Mrs. Anyone. Ever.

"Just a second," Greg said. "I have to get something in order to ask you this."

He got out of bed and as he put his hand in his dresser drawer to retrieve the accompaniment to his question, I screamed.

"Oh, Jesus, my neck," I said before I even thought about it. It was instinct. If I said no to him then this might be the end of what I considered a great relationship. Guys don't usually rebound from no very well.

"What?" Greg dropped an envelope he had picked up and ran to me. "My God, are you okay?" He touched my neck gently and I squinted to try to see what he had dropped. It was a thick envelope, but didn't seem to contain anything lumpy like a ring. I wondered if I could have been wrong and if there could be another important question he might ask that wouldn't involve decisions about changing my surname. At least my initials would stay the same.

"No, I'm okay now," I said, curiosity getting the better of me. "I'm sorry. I ruined your question."

"That's okay. Maybe I should not make such a big deal about it." He reached over the side of the bed and picked up the envelope. He passed it to me with a smile.

I opened it and saw a bunch of sheets of address labels, all with my name and Greg's address on them.

"Will you move in with me?" he asked. "I think we're great together and I love waking up with you."

My relief mixed with a smidge of disappointment. Okay, so, I didn't want to get married, but it would have been nice to be asked.

"You must be kidding me," I answered and Greg quickly looked hurt.

"Why?"

"Why? Why? Why do you think? My parents. My God, my parents would absolutely, totally die if I moved in with you. My parents are strict, strict Catholics. They make the Pope look like maybe he could try a little harder at this religion thing. Mom goes to Mass every day, not once or twice a week but every single day, seven days a week and twice on Sunday. Greg, my dad would sell everything he owns so he could charter a plane and come up and kill you himself if he ever heard we had sex, let alone that I had moved in with you. Hypocritical, I know, considering the whole 'Thou shalt not kill' thing and all, but in his eyes killing you would be better than me living in sin with you."

"But would you like to live with me?" he asked, unfazed.

"Yes, I'd love it. But, like I said, I can't. They would disown me if they knew."

"Then they don't have to know. Do they?"

Could he have been more perfect for me?

So, I moved into Mississauga and left a happy Rain to stay by herself in the two-bedroom that Clay's sugar daddy was fine with her staying in. We contacted Sugar Daddy in Tokyo and told him Rain would have to move out since she couldn't afford to stay there by herself and he agreed to pay more of the rent so she could stay on. He wanted someone he could trust to live there and I wondered if he would think the same if he ever laid eyes on her.

I moved my sparse belongings into Greg's apartment and knew I had made the right decision, even if it was something my parents could never find out about. But that was okay. I made Rain swear she wouldn't tell her mom the truth about our arrangement (just like we had both kept living with a gay guy quiet). I also had to remember never to piss her off in any way. It would be fine. Greg and I had started our lives together and, although it was cemented in a lie, I knew it was a beautiful thing.

The Long-Forgotten Sister

Dear Mom and Dad,

How are you? I am fine. And I have a new job. Actually, it is more of a lateral move. I am still at the same place, but I am now in charge of public relations for Hope House. I have even been on the radio. Imagine. I did great and I was relaxed. You would have been so proud. The radio people really liked me.

Beck says to thank you for the cookies you sent and our nice pink scarves you knitted for us. They are perfect. Beck doesn't wear anything else. Oh, I have started to date a guy. I mentioned him before. He was the vet who looked after Rain's cat. He asked me out after I went with Rain for a follow up visit with the cat and we have gone out two or three times. He is nice and quiet. I know, Nan always said to watch out for the quiet ones. Write me back soon. Give Taylor a kiss for me.

Love, Lisa

I had been working at the detox for almost three years, when I was interviewed on the radio. Someone at a local station decided booze was a snazzy, hot topic *du jour* and asked the manager for an interview. He shyly told them that he felt one of the front-line workers should do it, as we knew much more about the withdrawals that come with detoxification. He suggested me. I'm pretty sure my articulate voice and slow manner of speaking (yeah, right) had less to do with it than the fact that I had the initials "B" and "A" after my name and could lend a certain degree of legitimacy to the discussion.

I still don't know how I even agreed to do it. I was still the same person who dropped every course in university that required any kind of oral presentation until I was forced to complete one so I could get the one remaining course I needed to get my degree. I remember staying awake for nights before I had to do that presentation on Newfoundland's place in Canada. I had severe stomach issues and spent inordinate amounts of time in the bathroom during the two days before the big event.

I can recall so clearly standing bleary-eyed and pale before the class (about ten pounds lighter–a happy side effect–so looking pretty good, if I do say so myself). There was an annoying sound of rustling paper, so loud it was distracting me from my speaking. I was about to stop and ask whoever was making that racket to quit it when I realized that it was me. My hands were shaking so badly, the papers I held were rustling like leaves in a fall nor'easter. My voice shook even more than my hands and some people snickered. Suddenly panic set in and I couldn't breathe. I gasped and tried to continue. It was pathetic. But then, I focused on the material; on the topic that had so interested me. I spoke of when Newfoundland became a part of Canada in 1949 and how we had struggled to become a part of a country even as most of the residents of the island still felt they were in the country of Newfoundland. I spoke of the controversy surrounding the referendum that made us a part of Canada. I got through it, but swore it was the last time I would speak in public. Ha.

So, how was it that when my manager called me into his office one day and asked me to do a live radio interview on a station I knew thousands of people listened to, I agreed? The words came out and I immediately looked around to see who had said, "No problem," as casually and comfortably as if he had asked me to pick up a piece of paper for him.

As I left his office with the details of when and where and the general types of questions I could expect, I wanted to turn around and get on my knees to beg him not to make me do this. I walked up the long hall from his office to the OD and briefly thought about faking an illness or perhaps jumping out of a window from one of the upper levels of the building. Not to kill myself, mind you, just maybe to break an arm or a leg.

Arriving at the OD, I was faced with another problem. Christie, the bitch who hated everyone she worked with and me more than any of them, was waiting with baited breath to see why I had been called into Mr. Thompson's office.

She had a smirk on her face she didn't even try to hide as she almost sang, "So, what did he want? Are you in trouble again?" the last word accentuated with a broad grin.

I resisted ripping the smile off her face (although I think I could have physically done so) and smiled back. This would be a pleasure.

"Actually," I said, looking down shyly and trying to summon up a look of false humility, "he asked me if I would do a radio interview about alcoholism and withdrawal." I wished I could have lit a cigarette, taken a deep draw and sat back in a chair to watch the fireworks.

I had heard of people blowing their tops or exploding into a rage, but I had never seen it before. She didn't literally blow her top but she did explode, figuratively, at least. It started with the smile disappearing from her face to be replaced by lips pursed so tightly they started to turn white. Her face turned from a pale pink to a dark pink to a bright red as all the blood in her body seemed to rush there. I can't say smoke came out of her ears, but I pretended I could see it and smiled even broader.

"What?" she screamed and several clients came to the OD door to look in. One of the clients trying to sleep in the OD shouted for her to "Shut the fuck up!" after which she snapped at him, "You shut the fuck up, asshole." I was so gleeful at her reaction that I didn't see the icing on my beautiful cake standing in the doorway of the OD. There, taking up the entire width of the door and then some was Mr. Thompson. I could tell he'd heard what Christie had said. Her scarlet face quickly paled again as she realized the same.

Most of us swore on a client at some time. I'd done it once. I got angry from time to time and I was human. If someone spit on you or called you horrific names for hours on end, it was hard not to let loose yourself. Christie swore regularly on the clients and called them often hurtful names. No matter what, though, no one ever swore in front of the manager.

Mr. Thompson just stood there with his mouth open as two of the nosier clients in the house stood behind him tutting. I couldn't see them, but I could hear them saying "That's awful." and "That girl is terrible."

I fought the urge to squeal with delight and just turned to look at Christie who also had her mouth open quite wide. I took a mental picture. I wanted to be able to tell all my colleagues every minute detail of this moment; this wondrous, exciting, amazing, extraordinary moment.

Christie had appeared to be nice when she first came to work at Hope House. She was a nursing assistant and smiled at everyone, joked and seemed wonderful. And she was, at least until she got angry. Christie was a general pleasure to be around, but God help you if you said something to make her angry. The thing was that, along with Christie's ability to lose her temper in an extreme way, she also had the innate ability to get angry at the slightest little thing. Christie could misconstrue almost anything uttered by anyone; she would turn it into an insult or slight to her.

Working with her was like walking a tightrope. As long as you were ultra nice and super friendly all was well, but try to express an opinion contrary to hers or say anything you hadn't analyzed for possible misinterpretation on her part, and suddenly you were in the presence of Mount St. Christie. You just had to sit there as the volcano erupted all around you.

The worst blow up I had experienced from her was when I mentioned, in passing, a course I had done in university that included schizophrenia. Well, she went through the roof, accusing me of rubbing her nose in the fact that she didn't have a degree. I and all the staff and clients of Hope House, with the exception of management who only ever got to see the sweet side of her, suffered many more such eruptions. The staff soon took to swapping stories of her outbursts as a way of passing time in slow periods. One of my colleagues used to make up things to say to annoy her and rated her anger on a scale of 1 to 10, 1 being a slow boil and 10 being "burst a blood vessel angry."

"Christie, my office now," Mr. Thompson said in a voice much deeper than usual. He turned around and walked away.

A battle brewed inside of me. *Say it,* the evil, vengeful part of me said. *Go ahead and say it. Say I wonder what he wants. Are you in trouble?* with that same snotty voice she'd just used with me. The logical, sensible part of me told me to let it go, that I already had the opportunity to watch her squirming about her oh so big *faux pas*. It was one of those rare occasions when I almost listened to my voice of reason.

"Yup, interview on the radio. It's in two weeks. Well, enough chitchat, it looks like Mr. T wants to speak to you. You better run along, now."

Okay, so that was not really being big of me. It was not kindness, but I didn't repeat back to her what she had said to me mere minutes before. I thought that was somewhat nice of me. Suddenly the radio interview didn't look so scary. Nothing looked bad anymore.

Even though I had lots of time to prepare for my interview with the overtime shifts I and everyone else got during Christie's two week suspension without pay, I still felt unprepared on the day of my radio debut. Greg had been doing fake radio voices during pretend interviews for the past couple of weeks and I knew I could answer anything, at least if Greg asked it. Now, speaking to Johnny Wrench on WR03 morning talk might be another thing. I showed up at the station, dressed impeccably and superbly coiffed. Johnny Wrench wore a sweat stained T-shirt with a tear in the neckband and gym pants. Rain would have disapproved. I would have to remember to tell her later when I made my occasional call to see how she was. I still wanted to ensure she kept my little secret about my roommate.

"This is radio," Johnny said to me as he eyed my ensemble.

"No kidding," I answered. "Can't hurt to look decent, can it?" My instant dislike for him had a calming effect on me, as I was no longer thinking about my interview.

"Takes a lot more than the right clothes to make some people decent." Point to Johnny.

"So you just gave up trying," I snapped back.

"You'll be on after the news at the top of the hour. Here's a list of questions. I won't be asking them. We have a chick for that."

Awww, I'll really miss the opportunity to work with such a class act, I thought. A couple of minutes of silence passed before the door to the radio booth opened and Johnny introduced me to the chick. She was Dr. Delia Shaw and seemed out of place. She was quiet, shook my hand with a firm shake and then explained she had a Ph.D. in Psychiatry, but liked the radio as a forum for helping others. I saw Johnny roll his eyes before he spoke into the mic in a voice that sounded nothing like the one he had just insulted me with.

"Coming up after the news," Johnny said, "we have Dr. Delia Shaw and special guest Lisa Simms answering your questions about alcohol abuse."

Answering your questions? I had purposely not listened to this station since agreeing to the interview because I was afraid I would hear something that would freak me out. I hadn't thought about the possibility I could hear something immediately before air time that would do it.

"Is this a call-in show?" I asked.

The doctor looked wounded. "Why yes, weren't you told that?"

No, I had not been told that. I was told it would be a twenty-minute interview. When I told the good doctor this, she assured me my manager had been informed that this was a three-hour call-in show.

My throat closed. Three hours. Call-in. Anyone, anywhere, from the guy who had offered me an old sub sandwich he kept in the sleeve of his coat in exchange for my sexual favours, to the Prime Minister of Canada (not that I thought the PM was any better than sub man) could call in and ask me anything.

"I don't think I can do this," I croaked.

"Sure you can. I'm here and I can take over any questions you can't answer. If you are not sure of an answer just talk about something else you do know about. Most people won't even notice if you don't answer their questions. Think like a politician."

I did avoid certain questions like a politician and I was funny and quick and sounded well-informed. I surprised myself. It was as if some smart, cool version of me took over my body. I was in the groove and feeling good until, with about ten minutes left in the show, Delia took a call from a Christie. As soon as I heard Delia say, "Hi Christie,"

I could barely swallow.

"Well, Lisa, I would like you to tell us a little about yourself. How did you get this job at the detox?" Evil Christie said.

"Through the unemployment office. Then there was an interview and I got the job."

"And do you like the job?"

I had already spoken several times, over the past three hours, about the pros and cons of the job so I told Christie that, if I had not made it clear enough, I did very much like the job. I loved the challenge.

"But you lied to get your job, didn't you? I know your boss is listening and I think he would be interested to hear how you lied to him and told him that you had an alcoholic sister when you don't even have a sister. I bet he'd be surprised by that."

I flashed back several months to a night of drinking with Christie when she was still nice. She was the only other person on staff who was not a recovering alcoholic so I had relished the chance to go drinking with a colleague after work. A few hours later, I slurred out my story of the interview with Mr. Thompson to her, along with a few other stories of my life.

Delia was motioning across her throat in a cutting action to Johnny, who was in front of the board that contained all the phone lines. She obviously wanted him to end the call. Johnny just smiled.

"And I bet he would love to know how you fell asleep while you were supposed to be observing a client and the client left only to return with a big bottle of booze and a few joints which he shared with everyone there. How about..."

"Christie," Delia interrupted, "I'm sure our listeners will remember you from our many conversations and they are well aware of your struggles with delusions. I would like to ask my producer, Johnny, to go to commercial now while I confer with you in private and make sure you seek more in-depth help than I can provide on air."

Delia winked at me. I could have kissed her, but it was too late. Mr. Thompson might not have cared about my imaginary sister but he had held exhaustive investigations into the alcohol and drugs that found their way into Hope House. Everyone had stood behind me in a huge cover up and kept to their stories until the whole thing had eventually died away. Until that day.

The remaining three callers told me they felt sorry for me because Christie had made up such terrible lies about me. I agreed with them and told them it was all untrue. I was pretty sure I had lost my job, but I didn't want to give the place a bad name. They did help people, after all.

Irony is a funny thing. It is often cruel. But, it can also be hilarious; Christie got fired along with me for knowing what had happened with the contraband in Hope House and covering it up. Even more side-splitting was that management at the radio station offered me a job. I, the person who was afraid to stand up in front of thirty people in a university class, who talked too fast and had a Newfoundland accent, was going to be the host of the overnight show at WR03 radio. The station executives had liked my sense of humour and had received a lot of great response from listeners who called in wanting to hear more from me. I actually laughed when they called me to offer me the job. Of course, I jumped at the chance. Who knew what could be down that road?

The Big Surprise

Dear Mom and Dad,

How are you? I'm good. Missing you. Hope you're safe and sound. Well, nothing really new to report except that I have to say I love surprises and you got me good. Greg says hi. Kiss Taylor for me and take care.

Love, Lisa

I had become known as Lady Lisa. It was a stupid name, but my boss at WR03 had decided I shouldn't use my own name and I had to have something a little different for the overnight shift. Lady Lisa had to say smart, funny things and had to sound sexy at the same time. I also took calls from listeners as I played records, and my little *tête-à-têtes* with the callers were a hit. The nastier someone got, the more I gave back and the bigger the audience grew. It was quite freeing to speak my mind and never have to censor my thoughts. Well, except that no four-letter words were allowed on the air, but I could double entendre to my heart's content. I had become a bit of a celebrity in the months since I started my new on-air life and I had already gotten three raises since a couple of rival stations were trying to woo me and WR03 wanted to keep me. There were even posters around town that read 'Lady Lisa Loves Late Nights.' I was almost famous and could not believe it. Then again, no one had a clue what Lady Lisa really looked like so I wasn't exactly being mobbed or anything.

Greg hated it. Lady Lisa said rude and provocative things to people, mostly men, and there was no talk of any boyfriend in her life. Lady Lisa liked men and loved to party and told stories of debauchery all night long. I made up the most fascinating and exciting stories and I loved it. Lady Lisa was fun and fancy-free. I lived vicariously through her from midnight to six in the morning, Sunday to Thursday.

That was the other thing Greg hated and I agreed. The hours sucked. I only got to see Greg on weekends. The rest of the week, I pulled into the driveway in Greg's car and he walked out to get in it. A peck on the lips and it was off to bed for me; off to heal sick animals for Greg. In the evenings, we hung out, but I usually tried to nap between 7:00 and 10:00 so I could be fresh for the night and whatever lewd things it might bring.

So, we decided we would stay home every second Saturday night and make it our night. We listened to music, lit candles, drank wine, generally spent a little time in the throes of passion and just enjoyed each other. Saturday nights became sacred and the key to our relationship. All of our friends knew not to disturb us on a Saturday night unless the earth was about to crack open (and there was many a Saturday night Greg made me feel like it might).

So when the phone rang on one Saturday night, I jumped. I glanced at my bedside clock and saw it was 9:28. Greg, face full of whipped cream, asked me if he should answer it.

"Well," I answered, covered in whipped cream in places other than my face, "maybe this is not the best time. Let the machine get it."

Greg nodded and eagerly got back to a little Lisa Sundae we had created, complete with a cherry on top. The machine kicked in after four rings and suddenly my mother's voice filled the air.

"Not now," Greg said in a muffled voice to the machine.

But I, unlike Greg whose ears were covered by my thighs, could hear what my mother was saying. I pushed Greg off me and flew to the phone, grabbing it as my mother was saying, "Oh my, what are we going to do now," to my father.

"Mom, are you serious? You're at the airport? Here in Toronto?" I made a face to Greg who was already getting his pants on as he muttered the word 'fuck' over and over.

"Yes, my darling, we are here. Surprised?"

"Oh, yes," I answered, hoping my heart would slow down before cardiac arrest occurred. "I am really surprised."

"I know how much you love being surprised. So we are going to get a taxi to your apartment, okay?" She gave me the address to make sure it was right.

"No, Mom that will cost you a fortune. Listen, can you call back in five minutes so I can try to get a loan of a car and pick you up." I shot a look to Greg, knowing that I could just hop in his car.

"No, Lisa, that's okay. Dad and I have the money to get a taxi so we're coming there. Now, that is it. No discussion."

No discussion. The two words that meant the end to any conversation with my mother. No one ever talked anymore about a subject my mother had closed with "No discussion."

"Okay, see you soon," I said, solemnly.

"Can't wait," Mom said.

"Me too." I tried to sound excited, but felt too much like crying to pull it off.

It had been almost sixteen months since I had last seen my parents the Christmas before last. I missed them and wanted to see them, but they would be at my apartment in about thirty minutes or so and I had to get a fake job and a female roommate before they arrived. This was going to be a little difficult.

"Get out," I screamed at Greg as I threw his shirt at him then wiped the whipped cream off myself. "Get your suitcase now. Hurry."

I looked around and thanked God I'd been way overdue in doing the laundry. Most of Greg's clothes were with mine in garbage bags. He could take the whole works. But as I continued to look around, I realized there was too much of Greg in this apartment. There were fish mounted on the wall in the living room; a hideous painting of dogs playing poker in the dining room; a stereo system with speakers the size of most sofa chairs; the bathroom held Greg's towels with his initials on them (a gift from his parents); and a collection of model cars lived in a display cabinet against the wall. Suddenly, I knew this was not going to work. No way even I could pull this one off.

"Okay, what the Hell are we going to do?" I was almost crying. "We cannot pretend you don't live here."

"Lisa, we've been living together for going on a year now. Come on, let's just tell them. They will be happy for you, for us."

Oh, my poor, naïve Greg, I thought. You silly, silly man.

"You have no idea of the wrath of Mom; never mind Dad. You won't have to worry, Greg. You'll be dead. I, on the other hand, will have to listen to my mother tell me of my next life in Hell every single day for the rest of this miserable life. No one can lecture like my mom. No one."

While I was desperately trying to figure out what lie I could spin to my parents, Greg was unexpectedly on his knee in front of me.

"What are you doing?" I asked him. "Mom and Dad will be here any minute."

"Marry me, Lisa," he said softly as he held out a beautiful diamond solitaire ring. Marry me and I will make you an honest woman. I know this is not the best time and I had a big romantic thing planned for next week, but I want you to be my wife. I have never wanted anything so much. Please marry me." To my surprise, his eyes filled with tears.

I could have killed him. He had taken the most wonderful moment of my life and plunked it right down in the middle of one of the most frantic events ever. I had no time to enjoy it; no time to relish what would be the beginning of a whole new life for me.

I surprised myself by saying "Yes," and I kissed him. It was the sweetest kiss ever. I was going to marry this man and even though his timing wasn't great, I was sure I wanted to be Mrs. Greg Stagg more than I was sure of anything in my life.

"I love you," he whispered in my ear as he hugged me. We were both crying now and it all seemed like a sappy movie.

"I love you too, Greg, but I wish you would get the Hell out." My excitement about my engagement was surpassed only by my horrible fear at what was about to happen when my parents showed up.

"Lisa, we're engaged. They'll be happy. They'll be excited."

"They'll be homicidal. Trust me, you could give me twenty diamond rings, but unless a gold band and a service with a priest have gone along with it, then it won't help. We have to be married before we live together. Not close to married, not in love; nothing, only married in the eyes of God."

"Then we'll tell them that we are," Greg said. "We can say we got married and were waiting for the right time to tell them. We can say it was in church and everything.

I'll go next door and get a loan of their wedding rings. It will be fine."

I laughed out loud. He was in for such a rude awakening entering into my family. The only thing for my parents that could come close to my living in sin with a man would be me getting married without them. My father had talked about walking me up the aisle since I could walk and my mother already had a master list of invitees in my hope chest. I pictured my mother fainting at the news that I'd gone ahead and gotten married without her.

"No, that won't work. Look, I haven't got the time to explain the nuances of the neuroses that are my parents, but I promise I will fill you in some time before the wedding." Once I said it, I thought better of it and decided that maybe after the wedding would be a better time to fill Greg in. "We have to come up with a plan, fast. They'll be here in minutes."

"Say that you're house-sitting." Greg gave up trying to find a way to keep him in the apartment. "I'll go to Scott's for a few days and take most of my clothes." He started to empty his dresser drawers.

"House-sitting for who? And I told them I was living with some girl named Rebecca. Where the Hell am I going to find her in ten minutes?"

"That's it! I'm Rebecca's boyfriend." I shook my head.

"Okay," Greg tried again, "Rebecca has a cousin and you've been house-sitting for him. He's been in another country for the past year. And Rebecca is gone to visit him. You could say to them 'Isn't it too bad, Mom and Dad that you won't get to meet her?' Anyway, that will explain my stuff on the walls and everything. But I can still be your fiancé Greg (he smiled at the word and so did I) and I could still get to meet them."

Greg had a questioning look all over his face and my mind was whirling. Could this work? I told Greg to pack as I sat down and pondered the possibilities. I would need to give Mom and Dad our double bed and could put a lot of Greg's stuff in the spare room.

"Oh, shit," I said as I realized I had told my parents I was still working days at the detox. "I can't go to work at midnights and I can't tell them what I'm doing or they'll listen to the show. Can you imagine if they heard some of the stuff I say? Oh my God, I'm having palpitations just thinking about it."

"Well, take some vacation time."

"On such short notice? Besides, I don't have any vacation time built up yet. Haven't been there long enough. Damn."

"Call in sick."

Of course, that was the only choice I had, but this was radio and I was just starting to get popular so it would have to be a good sickness. It would have to be something dramatic. I pondered that for a bit and decided appendicitis might be good, but they might announce that on the radio, so I would have to settle for something less severe like an inner ear infection. Oooh, that was good. No, pneumonia since I would have to be sick for the duration of my parental visit.

"Call the station when you get to Scott's and tell them I have pneumonia and have to stay off at least a week. If Mom and Dad are here any longer than that, I'll have to call in sick again. Oh, Jesus, is this going to work?"

"My future in-laws won't have a clue that we live together. Now, I have to leave you, fiancé, and go sleep on Scott's sofa. You have his number, right?"

I nodded, then kissed him again and hugged him tightly. I loved him and I wanted him to stay with me because as long as he was with me, I felt everything would be all right. But I knew that for the next few days, I would pretend not to be missing the person I would miss most in the world, all while trying to keep my mother and father from knowing anything about my real life.

I did okay. It worked out pretty well. My parents seemed happy with my apartment and totally believed that Rebecca's cousin owned the place. They were delighted that I was getting married and Mom's plans for my wedding took up much of the visit. The one hitch in the whole thing came on the first night. I was almost asleep in the little bed in the spare room (I told them the double bed they were using was left over from when Rain and I shared a room at Clay's) when Mom came out to me holding up a pair of men's underwear.

"Lisa, these were in your bed," she said calmly.

For a second, I couldn't speak, but I knew any hesitation was an admission of guilt so I stood up and looked away for a second, pretending I had to turn on a light to see what she was holding.

"Yeah," I said, not sure of what the Hell I would say next.

"Well, why is a man's underwear in your bed, young lady? Is there something you need to tell me?" She put her hand on her hip in a move that instinctively made my blood run cold. That stance had never meant anything good.

"They're mine, Mom. Don't you keep up on fashion? Men's boxers are the most comfortable thing ever. You should try them." *Where in the name of God did I come up with that?* I wondered.

"Maybe I will," she said, smiling as she took the underwear back with her into my room. Phew, close call.

Dad wanted to take us out to dinner to celebrate our engagement, but I knew they'd saved up every cent they could spare to surprise me and there was not a lot left over. I told Greg this and he asked them out to dinner before they could extend the invitation to him and when we got to the restaurant, he insisted he pay the bill. When Mom said she felt bad about this I whispered, "He's good for it," and she smiled broadly. She then leaned over, whispered something to me and smiled again.

On the way out of the restaurant, Greg and I went to

the coat check to pick up our coats. As we made our way back to my parents, who were smiling at us while we walked toward them, I leaned over to Greg and quietly said six words that made him stop in his tracks.

"My mother is wearing your underwear."

She never knew the difference and they left Toronto, happy to see I was doing fine and that everything was going just the way I told them it was.

The Last Job

Dear Mom and Dad,

Can you believe it? I am really coming home. This is just too good an opportunity to pass up and even though it means sacrificing a great life up here, I have to take it. I can hardly wait. Of course, I will miss my friends and my wonderful job. I resigned my PR position at Hope House. I know it is hard to believe I got a job on the radio, but the station manager back home heard me interviewed on the radio up here and liked what I had to say. He said I had professionalism and sophistication. He also said that I was articulate. I have never been called articulate before. Can you believe that?

My flight leaves next Tuesday. I will see you then. Kiss Taylor for me and tell her I will soon be kissing her myself.

Love, Lisa

Out of the blue, I got a call that would change my life forever. The phone rang at 11:30 while I was running around trying to find something partially clean to wear to lunch with Paula, a girl I had met through Greg. She was Greg's assistant at his clinic and had been asking me to do lunch with her for weeks now. I finally ran out of excuses and was pretty much forced to agree to this visit with her.

Not that she wasn't nice; it was just that she was almost too nice in a fake kind of way. She always smiled and complimented me and always asked me if I had lost weight (who does not like that?) even if I had put on a few pounds. Paula was a hugger and would frequently hug me and then rub my arms and stand far too close to me while we talked. I liked to stand far away from people while they spoke and generally tried to avoid eye contact, if possible. Having someone standing four inches away from you tended to make it difficult to avoid eye contact.

The weirdest thing about Paula, though, was how she would never stop talking long enough to find the right word to use in a conversation so you ended up not understanding much of what she said. When she couldn't remember the word she was looking for she would just say "you-know-what" or "you-know-who" and keep right on going. This, even though you had no clue what "you-know-what" meant. So conversations with her would go something like, "…then John went over to the back of the you-know-what and took the cover off and helped you-know-who carry it over to his house."

The first couple of times I spoke with her I thought she was replacing crude words or phrases so I pretty much thought everything she talked about was pornographic. After I spoke to Greg about it, he told me she always did it. It caused quite a lot of trouble when she told people that Dr. Stagg had to perform an emergency you-know-what or that Fluffy had a you-know-what removed. Greg said he spoke to her about it several times and she didn't even realize she did it. She wasn't stupid, she just didn't take the time to think of what words she wanted to use. To her, I think the talking was more important than the content.

So, when I answered the phone that morning I was half hoping it was Paula calling to cancel. Instead, a strange voice spoke.

"Hello, may I speak to Lisa Simms, please." Now, everyone knows that when someone says 'may' and 'speak' instead of 'Is Lisa there?' it's someone or something important.

"Speaking."

"This is Brad Decker from CHCH 98.1 radio in St. John's. Have you ever heard of us?"

Duh. CHCH was the hottest FM station in Newfoundland. Well, at the time it was one of only two FM stations in the province. I listened to it all throughout university and knew the name of every host on it.

"Yes, I certainly have." What the Hell was he calling me for? Maybe they wanted to do an interview about my newfound celebrity in Toronto.

"Well, Lisa, we have heard a lot about you. Word gets back home, you know. We would like to offer you a position at our station, if you would be interested in coming back to Newfoundland."

"A position?" A job back home? My heart picked up the pace.

"Yes, we are looking for a new person to fill a slot in our morning show and we think you would be perfect. Of course, we'd like to have an interview and talk about salary and the like, which we could do over the phone. How does that sound?"

My mind started to catch up with my heart's pace as it raced along. I could get a job and move back to Newfoundland, but there was Greg and our apartment and his clinic. Of course, now that I could finally have a good job where I wanted one, I wasn't sure I even wanted to go there anymore. Damn.

I called and cancelled lunch with Paula and explained that something had come up. The head honcho at CHCH called me, as planned, at 2:00 and interviewed me. He told me he had heard Lady Lisa on a visit to Toronto and he thought I had the right combination of musical knowledge, zaniness, smarts and humour. He offered me a salary a little more than I was making at WR03. CHCH was FM and they could pay a little more than the AM station WR03 could, even in Newfoundland. It was also a morning show and that tended to pay more as well. So this was it. More money, back home. My heart sank at the thought.

I never thought anything could make me not want to go back home. It was home, for God's sake, and I loved everything about it. I loved the salt air, the salty roads in the winter, the snow, the rain, the wind, the people; even the fog. But I loved something more than all of that, it seemed, and its name was Greg.

So I told the guy on the phone that I would consider his offer and before I hung up, he upped it by a couple of thousand dollars. Why shouldn't such a hard decision be made even harder?

When Greg came home, I had cooked a pot roast for him (one of my few culinary specialties). It was a Thursday and as Greg was more accustomed to a tin of beans on a weekday than a scrumptious home cooked meal, he gave me an inquisitive look before he even took off his coat.

"Did you cook?"

I nodded.

"What's up?" he asked. "Paula was all upset because you cancelled lunch at the last minute. She said you told her something had come up, but I didn't know anything about it. She bugged me all afternoon to tell her what was going on. I called a couple of times and got a busy signal. Is something wrong?"

"Let's talk about it over supper." I had rehearsed how to tell him all afternoon, but I still didn't know what to say. If I made it sound too good he would insist I take it even though it would mean leaving him. Still, I had to make it sound good enough that he would understand if I did leave.

"Come on, Lisa," he said once he sat down to the roast and veggies. "End the suspense."

"I got a call from home."

"Is everyone okay?"

It was a logical conclusion that a call from home, which would incite me to cook a roast, would most likely be a bad call. In Greg's mind, someone was sick, dying, or dead.

"No, no, everything is fine. Actually the call was quite interesting." Yes, interesting, that was a good word, not great or exciting or amazing or scary, just interesting. "It was a job offer."

"In Newfoundland? Wow, what was it?"

"A job on the radio. Can you believe it? The station manager heard me when he was up here on business and he heard me say I was from Newfoundland, so he decided I would be perfect for the morning show on CHCH.

"CHCH?" Greg put down his fork. "That's FM. I love them. Wow, you'd be part of the sunrise team."

"Exactly." The sunrise team was three people who made up the morning show. The station manager told me I would be part of this three-person team, but I forgot to ask who I'd be replacing.

I told Greg more details about the job then the salary and he listened with a huge grin on his face. He was genuinely excited for me. He didn't seem one bit hesitant or sad that the job was in Newfoundland.

"What did you tell him?" Greg asked.

"That I had to think about it. I wanted to talk to you about it. I mean it will affect you, won't it. We will be thousands of miles away and that's not a great way to start a marriage."

He smiled. "Lisa, you have to take this job. You cannot say no. This is a once in a lifetime opportunity." He leaned back in his chair. "We can put the wedding off and do the long-distance thing. We're not in any rush. We can get married in two or three years and by then you'll know if the job fits or not or maybe you'll have enough FM experience that you'll be able to come back and get a better job here."

I watched as my ship of dreams sunk slowly to the bottom of my life. He was in no rush to marry me and seemed quite content to stay away from me while 'doing the long-distance thing.' He didn't even stop to think about it. He was completely fine with the idea of living without me.

I thought about Mom who was already picking out invitations and had booked the town hall in Ladle Cove for the wedding reception. Not that it would be a problem to reschedule the hall. Still, Mom had her heart set on July 14 of the following year. Truth be told, so did I.

Then there was after the wedding. Greg had talked about me going back up to Toronto. I knew that once I got out of this place, I wouldn't want to come back, especially if I was making a good living in Newfoundland. And how long would it be before Greg had some cute girl with a sick cat bat her eyelashes and thrust her cleavage at him?

I could see the fork in the road quite clearly. It did not merge. It was a choice–Greg or the job back home. If I picked one, I would lose the other. I wanted to scream and cry. But I didn't. I just sat there and tried to swallow the lump in my throat.

"You're okay with that, aren't you?" Greg asked. "Some things are bigger than even a relationship and a job like this is one of them. We'll see each other three or four times a year. I'll try to get down for Christmas."

I opened my mouth to tell him what I thought; to tell him that he was a mean bastard who didn't really love me or he would be upset like I was, that I was nothing to him and that if seeing me three or four times a year could do it for him then he didn't feel for me what I felt for him. Before I could get a word out, Greg laughed.

"Got you." He touched the side of my surprised face. "Lisa, I have a practice here and this great apartment and my friends and I would give it all away in a heartbeat if it meant I could be next to you. As it is, I know Carter would jump at the chance to buy out my stake in the clinic and St. John's can never have too many vets. We'll make a killing on the sale of the clinic and have enough to buy a house when we get home. I've been waiting for an opportunity to go back home myself and this is it. Now, call that guy and tell him you want the job."

And I did. Well, I did after I showed Greg how much I loved him and how happy I was that we were going to be returning home together. The pot roast got cold, but Greg didn't complain. The fork in the road became a straight line and I headed down it, knowing with all my heart that it was the right one, stepping forward without a doubt in my mind.

The End

Dear Mom and Dad,

Well, I am about to get on the plane and cannot quite believe I am coming home. I am so looking forward to the wedding and to my new life in my wonderful home. I will miss Toronto, but cannot wait to get home. See you soon. Don't kiss Taylor for me. I'll do that myself.

Love, Lisa

Six hours before my flight to Newfoundland was to leave, I was on the bathroom floor of my friend's apartment, swearing I would never drink again and crying because I didn't want to leave. I had a distinct sense of *déjà vu* and these feelings of apprehension surprised me. I was going home, to the rock. To the place I loved and ached for all while I lived in Toronto. Yet part of me was sad.

So much had happened since I came to Toronto. I was a different person than I was that day I set off for Hell. I was more confident, had done a lot–things I never would have believed I could and some things I wished to God I hadn't. I'd loved people who had since died and I had learned from all of it. I had hurt people and been hurt. Most of all, I had lost my innocence, I think. When I left Newfoundland the world was such a small place, just the area around my small circle of friends and family. Now the world seemed so much bigger. There was so much going on out there, all the time.

The party the night before consisted of light beer and pizza. I told a couple of the mainlanders at the party about the capelin I wished I had to roast and they loudly thanked God that I couldn't find any, and that they were not from Newfoundland. The idea of small, roasted fish at 2:00 in the morning did not appeal to them. I smiled and knew they could never understand.

Lying on the floor in Rain's bathroom that morning, I knew I had to get up the strength to go to the airport. I had said goodbye to everyone and knew that this was it. I had a one way ticket to Newfoundland. I would miss the people I came to call friends the most, and maybe, just maybe I would miss the city itself, just a little. It was like living with an annoying, overpowering roommate who infiltrated every part of your life but who you would miss just a tiny bit after you moved out.

I knew I would miss Jennifer, Kim and Pansy, but they were standing at my wedding, so I would see them soon. And I knew I would talk to them and write to them. I would miss Rain the most. She and I had developed some strange kind of bond, created in pain and anger and the kind of loyalty that comes from sharing sad and horrible stuff. We didn't talk every day, sometimes not even every month, but I knew she was there and she knew the same. I knew in my heart that this would not be the case once I left. We might talk from time to time or even write and I hoped she would go to my wedding, but we would never stay in close touch. The kind of bond we had could not be stretched too far without breaking and I knew the flight home would do the job.

I hugged her as Greg waited outside to drive me to the airport. To my surprise, she hugged me back. I might be wrong but I'm pretty sure she whispered "Love you" when she patted me on the back. I said "What?" to her, but she told me that she had said nothing.

"I love you, Rain," I said as tears filled my eyes. "Thanks for everything."

"You too," she said and I didn't know if she meant the 'I love you' part or the 'thanks' part. I prefer to think it was both.

Since Greg still had a few things to clue up and I had my job waiting and a new house to hunt for, I flew home by myself. We'd given up the apartment and he was staying with his buddy Scott until he flew home. He kissed me in front of the departure gate–a long passionate kiss.

"See you, wife to be."

"See you, husband to be." My cynical alter ego stepped outside my body for a minute and I watched her put two fingers down her throat in a feigned gesture of disgust. "I'll miss you," and I knew I would even though it would only be ten days until I saw him again.

I called Mom and Dad and told them the flight would be on time. They sounded so excited and could not wait to see me at the airport. It was June 25, 1989 and the temperature that afternoon in Toronto was a moderate 29 degrees, but felt more like 36. Not bad for Toronto.

I got on the plane and sat next to a man who was fiddling with his seat belt for about five minutes before he got it on.

"Going to Newfoundland?" he asked.

"Yes." I smiled even though this was a direct flight to Newfoundland and, therefore, a stupid question. "I'm going home."

"Been on vacation?" he asked.

"No, just going home." I turned away.

"So you're from Newfoundland?"

I nodded. Yes, hence the word 'home,' I fought the urge to say.

"I've never been, but I'm actually moving there."

"Oh," I said, thinking that perhaps I should try to belch loudly or something. Maybe that would stop his talking. *What was it with me and talkers?*

"I have a new job there," he said, "and it's a pretty big job. I guess I'm a little nervous about it all. You know; the move, the new job."

Yes, I did know. I knew exactly about moving to Newfoundland for a big, new job and it made me more than a little nervous to think about. I didn't need his to magnify my own similar doubts. I picked up the in-flight magazine and gazed at a cover picture of an up-and-coming French singer named Céline Dion. *Like anyone would listen to a French singer,* I thought to myself.

"The people are friendly, right?" the talker asked me.

Loaded question. The turning away had not quelled his need to share. Even my feigned interest in this boring magazine was not working. I was feeling very unfriendly yet I knew the reputation of Newfoundlanders–all welcoming and happy, invite you into their house for a cup of tea if they met you on the road and had never seen you before in their lives–but I was not that Newfoundlander. Surely I was not the only unfriendly one; surely not every person from home felt the need to listen to the incessant ramblings of every passenger on a plane. Still, I could colour this guy's view of my home province forever.

"Yes, in general," I said.

"Good."

He sat back and I was relieved. I had, not only once again saved the reputation of Newfoundlanders but, it seemed, had satisfied his desire to talk.

"So, tell me all about the place," he said, leaning toward me. The plane had not yet left the runway. I could be in for an all-talking flight if I didn't think fast.

"Look," I said, touching my stomach and screwing up my face. "I don't mean to be rude, but I am really not feeling well. I started my period this morning and the cramps are really bad."

I had learned early in my teenage years that any mention of 'womanly issues' could send men running from the room. I could get away with pretty much anything if I pulled the monthly-cycle card, which I had used and abused many a time. As always, it worked. Yes, I had probably told him a bit too much information, but he thought we were all friendly anyway. Maybe now he just thought we were a bit too friendly.

I closed my eyes and before I knew it had fallen asleep. The stewardess jolted me awake to tell me we would soon be landing and I wondered why she couldn't have told me after the fact.

The pilot announced that we were about to land. He told us that it was 14 degrees in St. John's. My seatmate shuddered and said "Brrr," but I smiled. This was home and everything would be okay now.

Throughout the years, I have often experienced that god of irony called Ha, the cruel teaser who always managed to lull me into a false sense of security. I had decided, with that last letter written to my parents from Toronto, that I would tell them only the truth from now on. I would write them letters from St. John's to Aspen Cove and I would really tell them how great my house was and who I actually lived with and how much I sincerely loved my job. That was what I planned to do.

But not everything goes as planned and I didn't want to worry them so the main thing is that I had intended to tell them the truth and if things had turned out that way, the way they had looked on that flight home from Toronto, then I never would have lied to them again. In the end, that's what counts. Isn't it?

ACKNOWLEDGEMENTS

There are always people in the background who encourage, support, advise, cajole, help, care, and see things in you that you can't always see. They made this book possible. Thanks to:

Kathy Skinner; Pam Hollett; Kim Wiseman; Ani Brinson; Elaine Duff; Marg Cumby; Terry MacDonald; Michelle Boutcher, Tree Walsh and Jean Anne Gollop of the AIDS Committee of Newfoundland and Labrador; Rebecca Rose; Tamara Reynish; Debbie Hanlon; Rhonda Molloy; all the girls at MLB and KIR; Maura Hanrahan; Paul Butler; and last, but not least, the Chaulks: Vince, Sam, Eugene, Shirley, Bert, Shirley (my other Shirley and other mom), Derrick, Tammy, Janice, and Kem.